Enough

Enough

Mary Jennifer Payne

orca soundings

ORCA BOOK PUBLISHERS

Library and Archives Canada Cataloguing in Publication

Payne, Mary Jennifer, author
Enough / Mary Jennifer Payne.
(Orca soundings)

Issued in print and electronic formats.
ISBN 978-1-4598-1330-4 (paperback).—ISBN 978-1-4598-1331-1 (pdf).—
ISBN 978-1-4598-1332-8 (epub)

I. Title.
PS8631.A9543E56 2016   jc813'.6   C2016-900534-8
                           C2016-900535-6

First published in the United States, 2016
Library of Congress Control Number: 2016931875

Summary: In this high-interest novel for teen readers, Lizzie has to protect herself
from her mother's boyfriend while looking out for her brother.

*Orca Book Publishers is dedicated to preserving the environment and has
printed this book on Forest Stewardship Council® certified paper.*

Orca Book Publishers gratefully acknowledges the support for its
publishing programs provided by the following agencies: the Government
of Canada through the Canada Book Fund and the Canada Council
for the Arts, and the Province of British Columbia through
the BC Arts Council and the Book Publishing Tax Credit.

Cover image by iStock.com

ORCA BOOK PUBLISHERS
www.orcabook.com

Printed and bound in Canada.

19 18 17 16 • 4 3 2 1

*To all survivors of domestic
and sexual violence*

Chapter One

If you could be granted any superpower, which would you choose? Would it be more fun to climb buildings like Spiderman, soar through the skies like a peregrine falcon, or run like a cheetah?

The decision wouldn't be hard for me. For the past three years, I've been wishing I could become invisible whenever Mom's boyfriend decides to use me as his personal punching bag. And tonight, as Dean's fingers close around my upper arm like a crab, digging into my flesh and making tears spring to my eyes, I make that familiar wish once more.

God, please make this stop. Please make me invisible.

Dean pulls me close and leans in so that his face is level with mine. Red, spidery veins crisscross the yellowy whites of his eyes like a subway map. At thirty-five he looks a good ten years older. His breath is hot on my face. He reeks of booze, cigarette smoke and sour sweat.

"You little bitch," he says, spittle landing on my cheek. I hold my breath, afraid of vomiting all over myself if I inhale his stench. "Where's my forty dollars?"

I stare hard at the front of his gray cotton T-shirt. The soft bulge of his stomach hangs ever so slightly over the waist of his jeans. Behind Dean, on the mantel of our fake fireplace, is a black-and-white photo of my grandmother when she was in her early twenties. It was taken at the waterfront. She's sitting on a rock, the wind blowing her thick, dark hair away from her face. Her full lips are pulled back into a wide smile. I have the same wide mouth and high cheek-bones. The photo is one of the only really beautiful things left in this townhouse. After Dad's death, the beauty in our family home steadily decayed, like a cut flower without water. Then Dean came along and made sure he destroyed any last remaining bit of beauty or sense of security that was left. He moved in three and a half years ago, and I hate him.

"What forty dollars?" I ask, forcing myself to meet his angry stare. "You're completely pissed. In fact, you probably spent it on booze or some whore and can't even remember."

His eyes narrow into snakelike slits. "If you want to be going to school tomorrow and seeing that prick of a boyfriend of yours, you better make them twenty dollar bills appear. Otherwise, you're going to have the 'flu' for the next week."

My head snaps back up to meet his gaze, and I laugh. "I don't have your money," I say. I'm shaking with adrenaline and fear, and I can only hope he doesn't notice. If there's anything Dean likes, it's weakness. I guess that's why he loves Mom so much. That and the fact that she drinks with him until they both become drooling idiots passed out on our couch.

"Think you're funny, Lizzie?" he slurs. "How's this for funny?" Suddenly his free hand is wrapped around my brown curls, and my head snaps backward. My scalp feels like it is on fire. For a brief second I'm scared my bladder is going to give out. If I piss myself, Dean will be in heaven.

But I won't give him the satisfaction.

"Yeah, I do think I'm funny," I manage through gritted teeth. "I'm funny, and you're pathetic. A pathetic loser and a waste of space." Then I purse my lips and spit at him. Most of the saliva misses him, but his chin ends up speckled with bits of foamy spittle.

Dean stares at me. I can almost see the wheels turning in his mind. Our fights have been worsening over the last two years. I've become more and more defiant and confrontational with him to ensure that all his anger is directed at me and not Charlie.

Then Dean does something completely unexpected. He smiles. It's a cold smile that doesn't reach his eyes. As his grip on my hair tightens, I realize I'm in trouble. Fear rises in my throat like vomit. I should've waited to come home. I knew Charlie had physiotherapy, but I was just too hungry to stay at the library any longer. Besides, I had no money to buy something to eat.

In the next instant, my world changes forever as Dean's thin, chapped lips press against mine. I struggle like a wild animal caught in a trap, but he's still ten times stronger than me, even in his drunken state. Walking me backward, he presses me up against the wall beside the fireplace. Tears roll down my cheeks as his hand fumbles under the fabric of my jean shirt. He pushes my bra up and begins to knead my right breast.

I know my grandmother sees what's happening. She's right there on the mantel, watching Dean do this to me. His free hand is now at the waistband of my black jeans, and he's undoing my belt. My blood turns cold. This can't be happening.

I try to move my head. It feels like my hair will rip out of my scalp with even the slightest movement. Dean moves his hips against me.

"I can feel you like it, you little whore," he hisses into my ear. "I've been holding back from doing this for too long. Your days of acting like a wild animal are over. You need some breaking in." I choke back a sob. I haven't even let Fahad touch me like this.

Please, Grandma. Please strike him dead. Do something. Don't let this happen to me. Make me invisible. Please.

"You knew this would happen," he whispers, his breath hot against my neck. His skin pushes against mine, faster and faster.

Tears roll down my face. I'm on a roller-coaster ride and it will end soon. It has to.

"When I saw you after your shower, wrapped up in your towel last week… I knew you wanted me as much as I wanted you. And I was right." His voice is breathless, strained.

I hear the click of a key in the front door downstairs, and a few seconds later the familiar sound of Charlie's heavy footsteps reaches my ears. Relief floods my body.

Dean stops and pushes me away. Then he roughly shoves me into the hallway and in the direction of my bedroom. I can hear the metal clinking of his belt buckle as he does it back up.

"Hey, darlin'," he calls out to Mom as I race into my room. "You home already?"

Shaking, I close my bedroom door behind me. Then I lean my back against it and press the palm of my hand against my mouth to stifle my screams.

Chapter Two

Dean moved in with us shortly after my twelfth birthday. He'd only been dating Mom for a couple of months, but there was nothing unusual about it. Within the first year of Dad's death, Mom began drinking. Then she started dating and was never without a man after that. She always invited the guys she was dating into our lives super fast.

When I went to the bathroom in the middle of the night, it wasn't unusual for me to pass a hairy, half-naked stranger Mom had brought home from whatever bar she'd been at. Usually he'd be too messed-up to notice me, but sometimes he'd give me a smile or nod. One time, this fat, bald guy reached over and tousled my hair like I was some little kid. I still remember the high-pitched yelp of pain he let out when I sank my teeth into his hand.

The string of guys Mom brought to live with us was mainly made up of losers who were about as intelligent as our dog, Trixie, but harmless enough. They'd either ignore my brother, Charlie, and me or try to become friends with us. They'd bribe us with candy and late nights watching television when we really should've been in bed. I knew they did it to get on our good sides in the hope of keeping Mom. We put up with them, mainly because we knew they'd be short-lived. After Dad died, Mom's commitment to anything beyond Charlie, me and booze disappeared. That included holding down a steady job, which meant we had to sell our house just off the Danforth. It was the only home I'd known. Charlie was even born there. It was so much nicer than the shitty, rented townhouse we now live in.

Things changed again when Dean came along. Mom was different with him. Whatever he wanted, she bent over backward to provide. Like Mom's, Dean's drinking got in the way of him holding down steady employment. He bounced between odd renovation jobs or late-night security jobs. With neither Dean nor Mom working long enough to bring in a steady flow of money, things were often tense. Mom still tried to be a decent parent to Charlie and me, but more and more, I was the one who made dinner, packed Charlie's lunches and helped him with homework. Now I'm even forging her signature on his school forms so he can go on field trips and stuff. One thing Mom has had to do is keep Charlie's physiotherapy appointments. This is super important, since he has really high arches and some sort of nerve damage because of the operation on his clubfoot. He has to wear a brace sometimes on his foot, and between that and the nerve damage, he is slow and unbalanced. At least she's always followed through with that.

I'm lying on my bed thinking about all of this while rubbing my lips over and over, until they are swollen and raw. The pain feels good—it helps dull the memory of Dean's flesh pressing against mine. I skipped dinner, though Charlie called over and over for me to watch *Glee* and eat fried rice with him on the couch. I feel terrible, because I never let Charlie down, but there was no way I could go out there and face Dean. I've always felt I am holding my own with him, that I've won as many of our battles as he has, no matter how many bruises I have to hide afterward. But not this time. This changes everything.

I stare at the ceiling, at the spidery crack from last year's leak that weaves its way across the entire length of my room. Spots of black mold are beginning to peek through the yellowed paint. Mom needs to know what happened tonight. Dean finally did something that will make her see what a prick he is. She deserves so much better. What she needs is someone like Dad. She needs someone good and kind who will love her and treat her the way he did, the way she deserves to be treated. Then she'll be able to stop drinking and go back to work as an ESL teacher. And Charlie will get the chance to have a real father figure in his life. Maybe Mom will meet someone who will be able to protect Charlie when he gets bullied about his disability, someone who will cheer from the sidelines at his soccer games. I close my eyes and imagine Mom's new boyfriend…he looks like a cross between Idris Elba and Brad Pitt. Someone kind of hot in an older-man way.

I'm imagining this fantasy man hoisting Charlie on his shoulders when my bedroom door swings open. Mom stumbles in. I breathe a sigh of relief. Now I can tell her about Dean.

But before I can get a word out, she begins to sob.

"Mom? What's wrong?" I ask, sitting up.

"Dean…" she stammers through her tears. "He…" She begins to rock back and forth, from one foot to the other, like a little kid who has just been punished.

I sit up. Has Dean done something to her? To Charlie? As far as I know, he only hits me, though he yells at Charlie a lot. My heart starts thrumming in my chest like a djembe. I'll kill him. If he's so much as laid a finger on either of them, I'll rip his beating heart out of his chest.

Mom points at me, her index finger shaking like a divining rod. Her dyed-blond hair is a mess. The top of her head looks like a bird's nest caught in a hurricane. "He told me…told me what happened." The words are slurred, but the hurt and anger in them are as clear as ice. "He told me what you did."

"What *I* did? Mom, he's lying…I didn't do anything." I'm pleading, close to crying now as well. "He grabbed me. He…" I trail off. It makes me feel dirty just to think about it. I can practically feel his hot breath on my face again, his fingers touching me…

"That's what he told me you'd say." She hiccups loudly. "How could you do this? He told me how you've been parading around in front of him in your bra lately when it's just the two of you here, pretending you didn't know he was home." A sob catches in her throat. "How could you do this to me?"

This can't be happening. I'm dreaming, and this is just a big nightmare. I pinch myself hard and close my eyes. All of this is like some bad *Degrassi* episode.

"Your father would be ashamed of you," she says, her voice hardening.

The words hit me like a gunshot. "Mom, please," I say. I'm crying just as hard as she is now. Snot mixes with salty tears on my upper lip. "You have to believe me. I hate Dean. You know I do."

Mom's face is a mask of fury. I can't believe this is real, that she is taking his word over mine.

"If anything like this happens again, I'm calling Children's Aid and telling them to put you in foster care," she says, her voice shaking. "You're not going to break up this family, Lizzie."

I stare at her in disbelief. Family? What a joke! We're hardly a family anymore. My heart hurts so much. Right now, not only do I wish I was invisible, I wish I was dead. If it weren't for Charlie, I don't know what I'd do.

My mind flashes back to my brother as a two-year-old toddler. He wasn't able to learn to walk like the other kids because of his clubfoot, so Dad would put Charlie's feet on top of his, and that way Charlie could feel the sensation of walking without falling over or worrying about getting hurt. We'd be at Cherry Beach, Charlie's high-pitched laugh ringing out like music as Dad walked him along the sand bordering the shimmering water dotted with sailboats.

I'd run alongside them, collecting rocks and bits of driftwood that Charlie could keep as souvenirs later. People would turn and smile, though I could detect the sympathy in their eyes. I wanted to run up and tell them they didn't need to feel sorry for Charlie, because he was going to be just fine. SickKids Hospital was going to fix his leg, but he would be strong and happy anyway because of our family. Later, as the sun began to set, Mom and Dad would barbecue hamburgers, hot dogs and s'mores on the charcoal grill, and we'd lay out a blanket and pretend we were medieval kings and queens having a feast.

"And another thing. You're grounded," Mom says, her words tearing into my happy memory. "No going out on the weekend, no seeing Fahad or your friends. For the next week you can stay in here when you're home. Dean needs a break from you."

I stare at her, tears still spilling down my cheeks. "*He* needs a break from *me*?" I choke back a laugh. "You *know* how he is with me, Mom. What's happened to you? Why don't you try being a mother again? Or would it hurt you too much to care about Charlie and me?"

My words hang in the air. Mom's face crumples like a week-old balloon.

As quick as a lightning flash, she's in front of me. "You have no idea what I've been through, Lizzie," she says, her voice barely a whisper. And then she draws back her hand and slaps me squarely across the face. My cheek burns like it's been splashed by acid.

I stare at her. "You are wrong," I say, covering the stinging skin of my cheek with my right hand. "*You're* the one Dad would be ashamed of." For the first time in my life, I realize I'm beginning to hate my mother. She's weak, and she's an alcoholic. Worst of all, she's placed

Charlie and me in danger with her addiction to men and booze. Basically, Mom's the biggest loser I know.

I turn my back on her and crawl into bed without bothering to take off my Converse. Without a word, I pull the comforter over my head. My bedroom door clicks shut a few moments later.

Chapter Three

It's five past twelve. I sit on the edge of my bed. My eyes are swollen, donut-like, from hours of crying. Once more I check to be sure my backpack is packed with all the necessities—toothbrush, makeup bag, a couple of pairs of jeans, some underwear, socks, my Ugg boots and two sweaters.

Am I really going to do this? Do I have a choice?

I slip a hand into the front pocket of my jeans and finger the two crumpled twenty-dollar bills I took from Dean. It's likely enough for a cab, but I'd rather not spend it all on that. Our townhouse is only a twenty-minute walk from Downsview Station. It's not too bad in the middle of a sunny, warm summer's day. But at midnight in the dead of winter, it's going to be a brutal walk.

I won't be able to leave if either Dean or Mom is still awake. Ninja-like, I make my way down the hall. The light from the television flickers like a beacon in the darkness, illuminating my way. I press myself against the wall and peer into our living room. They're both sprawled out on the couch, an empty bottle of Jack Daniels and a half-full bottle of Diet Coke sitting on the coffee table in front of them. Dean is snoring loudly, one hand stuffed down the front of his unbuttoned jeans. A shiny string of saliva leaks from the corner of his open mouth. I fight a very real urge to grab a knife from the kitchen and stick it into his chest.

Instead, I go and make a tomato-and-bologna sandwich for Charlie's lunch tomorrow. There's one juice box left and a slightly aged apple, so I add those. Then I scribble a note and place it inside his blue lunch bag before fastening the blue Velcro flap.

I love you, little bro. As soon as I am able, I'm coming back for you and Trixie. Love you like there's no tomorrow. X Lizzie

Trixie slowly hoists herself out of her worn dog bed near the front hall and comes silently padding over to me. Likely no one has taken her out tonight for a walk to go to the bathroom. I'm usually the only person who remembers in the evening. Her food bowl is empty, so I pour extra kibble in it. Then I put fresh water in her stainless-steel bowl. She looks up at me expectantly. I swear she knows I'm leaving her. I feel terrible. Charlie can't walk her, and Mom will only do it when she's sober enough to remember. I bend down and kiss her on the head, inhaling her pungent smell.

She whimpers and follows me to the front hall as I wrap my black wool scarf around my neck and pull on my jacket.

"I'm so sorry, girl," I say. The words stick in my throat. Trixie was here at the end of Dad's life. She was only a puppy, yet she lay beside him, unmoving, as he withered away. She provided him with nothing but unconditional love and warmth during his last days. And now I'm abandoning her. Her and Charlie.

I turn away from Trixie's soulful, brown eyes and try not to think of Charlie tucked away in bed, his brace propped up against the wall near the headboard. She softly whimpers at me. I don't want her to end up going to the bathroom inside. She's such a good girl and has always let me know when she needs to go outside. Besides, I'm not sure what Dean will do if he wakes up with a hangover and dog shit on the floor.

The thing is, if Dean or Mom wakes up before I can get out of here, I'm not going to be able to leave tonight. And I'm afraid if I don't leave tonight, I'll kill Dean. Or myself. Every nerve in my body is screaming for me to get out of the house now, but I put down my bag and grab Trixie's leash. For all the loyalty she's shown Charlie, Dad and me, I've got to show her some.

As soon as Trixie's outside, she runs over to the side of our unit and relieves herself. Wisps of steam rise from the hole in the snow her urine makes. She finishes and then sits down, despite the freezing wind. She stares at me, her eyes wide with sadness. "I can't take you. I just can't," I whisper into the blowing snow. Tracks of frozen tears line my cheeks. "But I'm coming back. Back for you and Charlie. I promise."

Still she doesn't budge, even when I walk back toward the front door. She's never done this before. Trixie is usually the most obedient dog, and I can't call for her to come because that might wake Mom and Dean. Instead, I go over and pick her up. She's as light as an autumn leaf, and she shakes in my arms. Somewhere down deep, I know her shaking is not just from the cold. It's like she has some sort of sixth sense about what I'm doing. After all, aren't animals always the first ones to abandon a ship that's going to sink at sea, or to predict disasters like earthquakes and tsunamis? They somehow know things we don't.

I get inside and gently place Trixie back in her bed. I'm just about to leave again when I remember something I need to take with me. I know I'm taking a huge chance, but I just can't bear leaving it behind. Carefully, holding my breath with every move, I go back into the living room. Mom and Dean are still passed out. I take the photo of my grandmother off the mantel, carefully wrap it inside my gray wool sweater and bury it deep inside my bag. Giving Trixie one last pat, I make my way downstairs and out the front door. As soon as I step outside, the bitter cold of winter bites at my exposed flesh and makes what I'm about to do real. I pull my scarf up farther to shelter my nose and chin from the wind. I pause. Snowflakes dance in the light of the streetlamp outside our townhouse complex.

I don't even know if Grandma will be home. In fact, I haven't seen her in nearly a year.

Taking a deep breath, the icy air stinging at my throat, I will myself to start walking. The newly fallen snow crunches under the rubber soles of my shoes. I try not to think about Charlie, about him waking up tomorrow morning and finding me gone. Most of all, I try not to think about him struggling to get ready for school without me.

Chapter Four

The subway car is quiet. I'm alone except for an older, red-faced man who is nodding off to sleep, a crumpled *Toronto Star* newspaper slipping farther from his hands with each snore. He looks harmless enough, but my heart begins hammering in my chest anyway. What if he wakes up and decides to attack me? I move to a seat under the emergency passenger-assistance alarm just in case.

I take my phone from my bag and check the time. It's already 12:35 AM. Nan will be asleep for sure, unless some reality television show has caught her attention. I'm not even 100 percent sure which subway station I need to get off at. I think it's Dundas. I know she doesn't live that close to the subway anyhow, that I'd still need to take a streetcar or bus to get to her place in Regent Park. But there's no way I'm going to try to find my way there at this time of the night. Thanks to Dean's money, I'll be taking a cab.

Half an hour later I'm standing in the cold, ringing the buzzer for Nan's apartment. My fingers and toes are numb. Unlike Nan's old place, where the entrance smelled perpetually like urine and the security cameras were blinded with black spray paint, this new place is relatively clean. The stainless-steel frame of the security system gleams. I catch my reflection in it. I'm a mess of puffy eyes and blotchy skin.

"Come on, Nan," I whisper. "Please wake up." I know she likes to have a glass of warm rum before bed, especially in the winter. If she did that tonight, she'll be sleeping like the dead.

The door behind me swings open, and two guys walk in. The first one is really cute and looks just a bit older than me. I'm thinking he's maybe eighteen. He's athletic-looking, with short dreads. The second one is taller and looks older. A black hoodie partially conceals his hair and face, though I can see glimpses of his face. His skin reminds me of the surface of the moon—all pockmarks and dents. He flashes me a creepy smile before I can look away.

Like a deer caught in headlights, I realize the danger I'm in a moment too late. As I try to move away from the dial pad of the building's intercom, the older guy steps in front of me. His lips draw back in a smirk.

"What's the hurry, little sista?" he asks, planting his arm against the wall. His arm is now a barrier between me and the front doors. I have no escape route.

All my saliva instantly dries up. My tongue sticks to the roof of my mouth. I'd usually have a smart-ass comeback, but the memory of Dean forcing himself on me earlier tonight is paralyzing me.

"Such big eyes," he says, leaning in closer. The smell of stale smoke wafts toward me. I stare at the deep lines that crisscross his face like train tracks, at the rough texture of his skin. His teeth sparkle. A gold grill covers his upper front teeth. He notices me staring at it.

"All the better to eat you with," he says with a wink, running his tongue along the smooth metal.

"C'mon, man, leave her alone," his cute friend says. "We got people waiting on us, and business to do."

Reluctantly he moves his arm, allowing me to run past the two of them and out of the building entrance. The cold night air hits me like a slap. I can hear their laughter behind me. My face burns. I'm furious. Part of me wishes I could go back and beat the ugly, hoodied one to a bloody pile of flesh with my bare hands. The other part of me knows it would be a really stupid move to even stick around. Guns and knives are as common as cell phones around here.

So I run. My sneakers crunch on the newly fallen snow with every step, documenting my escape. By the time I reach my destination, my breath is burning in my chest. It's a twenty-four-hour Tim Hortons two doors down from Grandma's building. I slam through the doors, my bag bouncing against my back, and throw myself onto one of the chairs at the nearest empty table. A massive Santa holding a coffee is plastered onto the window beside me.

A group of middle-aged Muslim men glance up at me from their tea and conversation. I raise an eyebrow defiantly back at them. They look away and begin talking again.

What the hell have I done? I've got classes tomorrow, and a biology exam on Thursday that's super important. I glance at the clock. It's nearly one thirty. How is Charlie going to feel when he wakes up and realizes that I'm gone? First Dad disappears from his life, and now me.

I lay my head on the table, trying to figure out what to do. There's no way I can go home tonight. Besides, I'm not going back if Dean's there. Ever. Tears roll down my cheeks, and I pull my hoodie over my head. No one's paying attention to me in here anyhow.

There's a large woman in a motor-ized scooter sitting at the table beside me. A small dog with long hair tucked away from its face by a pink bow sleeps at her feet. The woman's gray hair is also carefully styled, and a brightly colored silk scarf sits neatly tied around the crepe-papery skin of her neck. I watch as she works away at a cross-word puzzle. I wonder why she's here in the middle of the night. Does she have any family? Is she homeless? Would anyone miss her if she was gone? It's obvious she's still got pride and is trying to look as good as she can.

Homelessness is something I've been afraid of since Mom began drinking, especially when she started getting fired from jobs. Between the welfare checks she and Dean collect, there's enough money to pay rent, though food gets pretty scarce at times. I've gone to the food bank with Mom more times than

I'd like to remember at the end of the month, and Fahad even bought food for Trixie a few times until we discovered a food bank for pets near Jane and Finch.

Fahad. My stomach turns at the thought of him. I pull out my phone and, before I can stop to think, dial his number.

After five rings he picks up. "Lizzie?" His voice is fuzzy with sleep.

"I'm sorry," I say. "I had to call." I pause. What am I supposed to say now? *Hey, Dean tried to get it on with me tonight. And guess what? He got further than you ever have.*

"It's two o'clock in the morning. I've got a math exam tomorrow. What's going on?"

"I'm…" The words stick in my throat like peanut butter and crackers. "I'm not going to be at school tomorrow."

"What?" I can tell he's super-annoyed now. "Come on, Lizzie, seriously? You woke me up to tell me that?" I would be pissed too if I was called in the middle of the night for such a lame reason.

High-pitched voices erupt in the background. Fahad covers the phone. His hand rubs against the receiver, creating muffled static in my ear.

"It's just Junaid, Mom. For God's sake, don't have a fit. Do you want to talk to him?"

Despite having dated Fahad for a year and a half, his parents have no idea I exist. They'd really lose it if they discovered that not only was he dating a non-Muslim girl, but also one that's half black at that. His father's joining in on the shouting now.

"Give me that phone! Let me see Junaid's number. By God, hang up and I'll ring him back right now!"

I quickly end the call and turn off my phone. It was stupid to call Fahad at this time of the night. Am I losing my mind? His bedroom is right beside his parents'. He's going to be so mad at me.

A tall man with dirty, gray hair down to his shoulders bangs through the doors. He stands in the middle of the coffee shop, scanning the room, hands stuffed deep into the pockets of a long black trench coat.

"Effin' terrorists," he says, spittle flying from his mouth. I cringe. He's looking directly at the table of Muslim men.

They look up, then quickly away. I can tell they wish this freak would disappear, melt into the floor, and not give them any trouble. I feel the same way and make a point of staring closely at my nails. There's a half-moon chip out of the careful baby-blue manicure of my right thumb.

I smell him before I see him sit down across from me.

"Hi, pretty baby," he says. Black stumps that were once teeth smile at me. The smell of dead rodents wafts across the table. Instinctively I cover my nose with my hand.

"Cat got your tongue?" He reaches for my free hand. I pull it away before he can touch me.

"I need you to leave me the hell alone," I whisper through gritted teeth.

He frowns at me, and I notice something crusty hanging from his left eyebrow.

"C'mon," he says. "You know you want it."

"What I want is for you to LEAVE ME ALONE!" I yell. My entire body is shaking like I'm having a seizure. Suddenly it's Dean in front of me. Everything I wanted to say, everything I was thinking earlier tonight, comes flooding back. Tears stream down my cheeks.

A dark-suited security guard moves toward us.

"You heard her, Harold." The woman on the scooter is suddenly beside me. I didn't even notice her approach our table. "Now leave this young lady the feck alone or you'll have to contend with me. And I'll make sure you don't get a space at the shelter for the rest of this long, cold winter."

She nods at the security guard. "Throw him out if he doesn't get his bloody ass the hell off of that seat in two seconds." As if in support of this, the little dog at her feet yelps.

Harold stands up, slams his hands down on the table and scowls at the woman. Still, he silently sulks away from us without another word.

"I'm Maie," the woman says, reaching out to shake my hand. She's wearing fingerless lace gloves, and her nails are painted bright silver. I notice her accent. Her voice is like Robert Patterson's, but rougher. It's like she swallowed gravel for supper. "Don't mind Harold. Though he doesn't seem it, he's harmless. Just hasn't been right in the head since his tour of duty in Afghanistan."

"You're from England," I say, feeling completely stupid as soon as the words are out of my mouth. I'm stating the obvious, but I'm just too tired to think straight. And I don't want to talk about Harold. If he's screwed-up from joining the army, too bad, so sad. It doesn't give him the right to terrorize me.

"I'm from England." Maie laughs, a deep throaty laugh. "And you?"

"Oh. I'm Lizzie. I'm from here... from Regent Park."

She frowns, causing deep lines to appear between her eyebrows. "No, you're not. I know everyone here in the Park. And if there's one thing I don't like, it's liars." Her expression hardens, and I know I've made a mistake by lying.

However, I'm not stupid enough to go around telling people my business. Even though Maie helped get insane Harold away from me, I don't know her. It makes me nervous to tell anyone too much about my situation. I'm always afraid that Children's Aid will be called if anyone finds out what it's like for Charlie and me to live with Mom and Dean.

"Actually, it's not a complete lie. My grandmother lives here, so it's like a second home to me." I don't tell her I've been down here less than ten times in the past two years.

"Living in the Park and visiting the Park are like chalk and cheese." Noticing my confusion, she quickly adds, "It is a completely different experience altogether. Who's your Gran anyhow?"

"Rose Duncan. She lives around the corner. I tried to go to her place before coming here."

A wide smile spreads across Maie's face. That's when I notice she's missing several teeth on the left side of her mouth, which has left the remaining ones leaning like dominoes. Though her eyes are a startling blue color, the bottom lids sag like a hound dog's. She looks a lot older than Nan.

"You're one of Rosie's grandchildren? Why didn't you say so? Can you believe this, Chester?" This time there's no response from her dog. He's curled up again, fast asleep at her feet. She looks back at me. "Rosie's flat is just two doors down from mine. You'll come back with me until the sun is up and it's a decent hour to wake your Nan."

I raise an eyebrow in surprise. I thought for sure Maie was homeless. Shows me not to stereotype people. Anyone seeing Mom on her worst days, when she's been drinking heavily and can't be bothered to shower or put makeup on properly, would likely think she's homeless too.

"Can I ask you something? Why are you here at this time of night if you have a place to sleep? A home?" I pause, hoping I haven't offended her. "Not to be nosy or anything."

But rather than being offended, Maie laughs, revealing the black gaps in her mouth again. "I come here to be around people. Got insomnia, I do. Rarely sleep more than two hours a night in my old age. This is better than sitting in my apartment with only a television in front of me. Rather be around real flesh and blood. Not discounting Chester here."

She leans over the table closer to me. "But the real question is why *you're* here in the middle of the night, Lizzie."

The smile disappears from my face. "Do you mind if I don't explain it right now? It's a long story, and all a bit fresh."

Maie nods. "Let's get you to mine for a few hours of sleep. If there's anything I understand, it's needing to keep our secrets close to us sometimes."

Chapter Five

I curl up on Maie's couch under a wool blanket that smells strongly of moth-balls and cedar. The smell tickles my nose, causing a volcanic eruption of sneezes. The apartment is small but cozy and warm. There are photos every-where—on the mantel of the fake fireplace, on the lace-doily-covered side tables and on the shelves of a towering entertainment system. Some show a young, slim Maie with red-stained lips posing with a good-looking man and a little boy. Looking at these photos and then thinking of Maie in her wheelchair with just Chester for company makes me sad, though I am sure she wouldn't want my pity.

As soon as I close my eyes, Dean's face swims into view. My entire body begins to shake, and I end up staring into the darkness for what seems like forever trying to stay awake. I'm afraid to go to sleep in case I end up dreaming about what happened. I can't believe Mom brought someone like Dean into our lives. And what really blows my mind is how she's taking his story over mine. Am I that worthless to her?

Curling up with my legs tucked to my chest, I stare into the inky darkness of Maie's living room. I wish there were some way to go back in time, to have our family together again. But I know that is both childish and stupid. Life is not like the movies—not everyone gets a happily-ever-after ending.

At some point I drift off to sleep, though it couldn't be for more than an hour or two. Maie wakes me up by opening the heavy curtains that cover the living-room windows. Bright sunlight streams into the apartment, jolting me awake. I sit up, feeling heavy and disoriented. It takes a few moments, but then every-thing that happened last night between Dean and me crashes back into my memory like a tsunami. I feel dirty in a way that I know no amount of soap or showers will cure. My life is suddenly surreal. Here I am in this strange woman's home and no longer welcome by my mother in my own. Darkness washes over me.

Maie presents me with a steaming cup of milky instant coffee. "Good morning, Lizzie."

"Good morning. Thank you," I say, taking the mug from her hands. My eyes feel like someone's dumped about a million pounds of sand into them.

"I'm going to go across and get Rosie," Maie says as I sip away at the coffee, trying not to scald my tongue. "I take it she might not know you're coming?"

I nod. "Yeah. I definitely think it will be a surprise."

Less than two minutes later, Nan sweeps into the room. Her long dreads are curled up on top of her head and tucked under a brightly colored woven scarf. Gold hooped earrings dangle nearly to her shoulders. At nearly six feet tall, she towers above Maie. She rushes across the room, wraps me in her arms and gives me a massive, bone-crushing hug.

"My lovely Lizzie," she says. The smell of vanilla and jasmine envelops me. I feel safe for the first time in a long time.

Nan lets go of me and sits down. Her eyes carefully scan me from head to toe, taking in my tangled hair, red eyes and ashy skin. Concern sweeps across her face. For a moment I see my father reflected in her eyes, in the way she holds her chin up proudly.

"What happened?" she asks.

I can't lie to her. She'll figure me out in a second. Though she's met Dean less than a handful of times, I know she doesn't approve of him or of Mom's behavior since Dad's death.

I twist Maie's wool blanket around and around my right index finger. How am I supposed tell Gran what happened with Dean? If I tell her everything, we'll be on the subway in two seconds flat, on our way back home so that she can kill him with her bare hands.

"Things got really bad last night." My bottom lip trembles. Don't cry, you stupid baby, I think.

"How *bad* is bad?" Nan asks, leaning in. Her eyes are dark pools of seriousness. She takes my hands in hers and holds them tight to stop my shaking.

I pause, remembering what Mom said to me when she came into my bedroom. The look on her face haunts me. I'm so afraid she'll hate me forever if I get Dean arrested, if I split up *our family*. What I need to do is somehow get Dean to slip up so that Mom can see he's lying. But I'm not sure how to do that just yet. At the moment, I want to be as far away from Dean as possible. And I want Mom to stop hating me.

"Dean got super angry and pushed me. Hard." I look Gran in the eye as I tell her. It's not a complete lie. More of a half-truth.

Nan gazes at me intently, her eyes darkening with concern. She knows I'm not telling her everything.

"What do you need me to do?" she finally asks, releasing my hands. "I can talk to your mother, phone Children's Aid…or you can stay with me for a while." Standing, she walks over to the window and looks out at the bright winter day before turning back to me. "The thing is, Lizzie, I don't have the space or the money to take in both of you. But I need to know if Charlie is safe there with that *man*."

"Dean's never lifted a finger toward Charlie. I mean, he's shouted at him a couple of times, but that's it." I don't add that the yelling was when Dean was drunk, and that Charlie hadn't done anything other than maybe stumbling and knocking into something. Sometimes all it took was turning the television to a program Dean didn't want to watch. Is Charlie safe without me there? After the way Mom turned on me, I'm not sure. One thing I do know is that I don't want Children's Aid to step in. If Charlie and I were put into foster care, we might get split up.

There has to be a way Nan can take us both in. I'm almost old enough to get a part-time job. Maybe I could make enough to cover at least part of the cost of Charlie and me living with Nan. If not, Dean has to go. And then Mom needs to get clean, so she doesn't bring home any more losers like him. Most of all, she has to get a job again.

"You'll need to register for school down here," Nan says. "If you're planning on staying down here any length of time, that is. Or else you'll have to travel all the way back to your school daily."

My head is spinning. If I transfer my credits to a school down here, I'll hardly ever see Fahad, if ever. Just the thought of that leaves a heavy sickness in my chest. I'm so used to hanging out with him every day at school and usually after school. Being with him allows me to escape my home life, if only temporarily. We've been together for nearly two years. I also don't have a lot of close girlfriends other than my best friend, Maria, mainly because there are not a lot of people I trust. I do a pretty good job of covering up what my home life is like by getting good grades and making sure the laundry is always done for Charlie and me. Once, when we ran out of laundry soap for a couple of weeks, I hand-washed all our clothes in the kitchen sink using a bar of Irish Spring.

The other reason why I don't have a lot of friends is because I spend so much time with Charlie. While other girls my age get together on weekends to shop or hang out in their bedrooms, talking about boys and music, I'm watching television or playing Xbox with my brother. It's not easy to make friends when you never have any time to socialize with them. Maria is good that way. She's more into books than clothes and spends a lot of time helping out at home as well. Her mom and grand-mother came to Canada from Honduras just a few months before she was born, and neither of them really learned much English, so Maria has to do a lot of translating at doctor appointments and stuff. Her mom was diagnosed with MS a couple of years ago and still struggles through her job as a cleaner at some of the big office buildings downtown. I know Maria is worried a lot about what's going to happen when her mom can't work any longer. She and I under-stand each other. We're both caretakers at home, but for different reasons.

"I think I should try to stay at Roseview," I say, taking a sip of the coffee. It's bitter and strong. "I'm doing pretty well, and I have a transit pass from Pathways, the place I go for free tutoring. It would be hard to leave school in the middle of the year."

Nan nods. "If that's the case, you better get going to brush your teeth and have a quick wash. You'll have to wear a pair of my knickers. Because you're not going out with dirty ones on."

I nearly choke on the coffee. "Oh my god! I've got some underwear in my backpack."

"Don't take the Lord's name in vain, Lizzie," Nan says. She raises an eyebrow at me, but a small smile tugs at the corners of her mouth. "You're going to be late, so I'll write you a note. Just how many of your bits and pieces did you manage to pack into that backpack?"

"I have enough to last for at least two changes of clothes," I say, handing Maie back the mug. "Thanks so much for everything." I'm suddenly hit by the realization that she didn't have to do all of this. In fact, most people would've left me in Tim Hortons to deal with things on my own, not brought me into their home. I'm pretty sure I wouldn't have done what Maie did.

"My door is always open for you," she answers. "And you're most welcome."

As we leave, Nan turns to me. "We'll meet at your house at three thirty sharp this afternoon to get more of your things and to tell your mom you'll be staying with me for a while."

My heart plummets. What if Dean's there? As we walk down the hallway toward Nan's place, I stare at her strong shoulders. She holds her head high and walks like a queen. I smile and tell myself there's no way Dean would dare try anything with her around. I just hope I'm right.

Chapter Six

Something's wrong with Fahad.

It's taken me a full hour and a half to get to school. I had to take a streetcar, the subway and a bus to get here. By the time I go to the office to pick up my late slip, it's already transition time between second and third period.

I find Fahad at his locker. His dark hair is carefully spiked, and comfortably worn jeans sit low on his waist. His back is turned to me as he grabs his textbooks. The sight of him makes me feel better, but I'm also drunk with nervousness. I can't get what happened with Dean off my mind—it's like the experience is tattooed onto my soul.

I wrap my arms around his waist. "Surprise," I say, my voice thick with false confidence.

Fahad stiffens. It's just for a fleeting second, but there's no mistaking it. I feel the muscles in his upper back and shoulders become as hard as rock at the sound of my voice. It's like I'm hugging an ironing board.

He turns to face me. "Hey, Lizzie. I thought you weren't coming today." His smile is forced and tight.

"Yeah, well, I didn't think I'd be here either. And I'm so late, I haven't even been to class yet." Out of the corner of my eye I see the hall monitor moving toward us. We need to get going.

"My parents are really pissed, you know," Fahad says, closing the door to his locker and snapping the lock shut. "Now they're talking about arranged marriage within the next four years. What were you thinking, calling in the middle of the night?"

"I…" My face burns like asphalt on a sunny day. What can I say? It was completely stupid of me to call him like I did. He knows it, and I know it.

"There were some problems at home last night. I couldn't sleep," I finally say.

He eyes the hall monitor. "It's just too much, Lizzie."

"I'm sorry. I know it was a mistake. It won't happen again." He's not looking me in the eye. Panic claws at my throat like a wild animal. "I swear it won't."

"My parents called Junaid. And his mom and dad freaked out because he was fast asleep. They thought someone had died back home when they got the call in the middle of the night." Fahad stops talking and finally looks at me. His expression is emotionless. "When I said it's too much, I meant it. I can't do this anymore, Lizzie."

I stare at him. I'm a fish out of water, suffocating with panic. "Please don't do this." My voice is barely more than a whisper. "Last night, Dean…he…"

Fahad doesn't even let me finish. "Yeah, I know your life is hell with Dean, but I just don't want to deal with it anymore. I'm done."

I open my mouth, but no words come out. Instead I watch, slack-jawed, as Fahad walks away from me and down the hall to his next class. As soon as he disappears around the corner, I turn and run out the nearest exit. The cold air stings my face, and I nearly slip on the icy stone steps of the school, but I don't stop running until my legs and lungs burn so badly I can't go on. I collapse on a nearby park bench, huge sobs racking my body.

When I think back to what happened last night, I want to die. Another person touched my body in a way that only Fahad should. Maybe Fahad would think I did something to deserve Dean doing that to me. Maybe he'd blame me like Mom did.

The thing is, Fahad doesn't even know what happened with Dean. The truth is, he just doesn't want to be with me. Period. He doesn't want to deal with my screwed-up, alcohol-fueled family drama anymore. And I don't blame him, because I don't want to deal with it either.

I sit on the bench as a light snow begins to fall around me like dandruff. My bum becomes numb from the cold. Car after car whizzes by. I can't help wondering what the lives of the passengers inside are like. Are they on their way to business meetings, or to meet friends for lunch? Maybe they're heading to the hospital to say goodbye to a dying relative, or home to a loving, happy family like the one Charlie and I used to be a part of.

Eventually, the cold begins to numb my feet and fingers to the point where the pain is unbearable, despite the wool mittens Nan gave me to wear. But that pain is nothing compared to the deeper hurt spreading through me. After years of fighting to keep Charlie safe from Dean, and struggling to do well in school despite everything going on at home, I feel like I've fallen down a deep hole. For the first time, I have no hope of a way out. Even Mom and Fahad have turned away from me. I've had enough.

Chapter Seven

I know Nan will be right on time, so I make sure I am as well. One of Nan's biggest pet peeves is people being late. She always says it indicates a lack of respect for whomever they're meeting. And even though the thought of returning home makes me sick with anxiety, the novelty of hanging out at Pizza Pizza in the strip mall near school wore off after a few hours. I spent the entire time drinking Diet Coke like a junkie while staring at the silent television screen attached to the wall. It was stuck on a channel that plays local, breaking news over and over. I tried not to think about the split with Fahad or about what happened with Dean. Instead, I attempted to focus on the man who drowned yesterday trying to save his black Lab from the Don River (the dog managed to pull itself out of the river, unharmed) and on a daylight shooting at a busy restaurant in the Yorkhill Mall. But, of course, it didn't work. I tried to get hold of Maria, but her phone was turned off, so I just texted her, saying things are really bad with Dean and that I'll be away from school for a couple of days.

At one point, I broke down and ran to the bathroom to bawl my eyes out. The cashier and two guys cooking pizza didn't say anything, but I caught them staring at my swollen, blotchy eyes as soon as I sat back down at my table. Then I made the stupid move of texting Fahad but got no reply. I know he checks his phone constantly, even in class. It's hard to believe he's really cutting me completely out of his life after one mistake. It was just one phone call. And it's not like it's my fault my home life is completely effed-up.

Head down, hands stuffed in my coat pockets, I turn the corner and step onto my street. I glance up toward our house. Nan's already standing out front, waiting for me on the sidewalk, in her long red woolen coat. Nervousness sweeps over me.

What if Dean's home? And what if he lies to Nan and tells her the same lies he told Mom? I don't think she'd believe him the way Mom did, but then again, nothing in my world seems to be happening like it should.

I wave to Nan. Maybe this is all a bad dream. Maybe I'm going to wake up to find everything the way it usually is. That gets me thinking about Fahad again. A heavy, burning hurt spreads through my chest. All of this can't be real. It just can't be.

By the time I reach Nan, I'm dizzy with anxiety.

"Now, I think it's best if your mother and I speak about all of this ourselves whilst you are gathering your things," she says matter-of-factly as we make our way up the concrete walkway. "Is she still drinking heavily?"

I nod. It would be stupid to lie. In fact, there's a good chance we'll walk in and find that Mom's a slurring, stumbling mess already. Charlie has no physio appointment today, and he gets bused to and from school. That means nothing's standing in the way of Mom and her big bottle of Jack Daniels at the moment.

Charlie. My heart sinks. He'll be home any minute.

Nan rings the doorbell before I can slip my key into the lock.

"It's just polite to give your mother a heads-up that you're not alone," she says, seeing the confused look on my face.

I understand. Mom and Nan used to be close when I was younger. I remember Nan teaching Mom how to cook curried goat, roti and callaloo at our Thanksgiving and Christmas celebrations. Their laughter would ring out from the kitchen, and afterward we'd all sit around the fireplace, singing carols, ripping open presents, and eating creamy yellow curry and drinking spicy eggnog until our stomachs were ready to burst.

My vision blurs with tears. There will never be another Christmas or Thanksgiving like that. Last year Mom and Dean served us an overcooked turkey they'd gotten free at the local food bank. The meat was so dry it tasted like sawdust, but Charlie and I ate it anyway because we were so hungry. Mom made us wait hours while she cooked the bird until it was nearly ashes in our oven. Then she served it to us with soggy McCain's French fries while she and Dean consumed a liquid dinner. This year there's not even a Christmas tree up yet. I told Charlie I'd get us one by the weekend if Dean and Mom hadn't yet. That's why I took the forty dollars from Dean in the first place.

We wait another couple of moments, and then I unlock the door for us and we step inside. Maybe I'll be lucky enough to avoid Mom and Dean after all.

Nan and I take off our boots in the bottom hallway and walk upstairs. I let Nan lead. My body feels disconnected from my mind. I'm walking roboti-cally. The only thing that calms me is the knowledge that soon I won't have to deal with any of this anymore.

The living room is quiet. Though it seems no one is at home, it wouldn't surprise me if Dean or Mum is passed out in their room. Nan looks around and clears her throat.

"Go grab your things," she says, surveying the room. The coffee table is littered with the usual empty cans of Coke that Dean and Mom use for mix. A half-smoked joint sticks out from a cracked glass ashtray.

I nod and head down the hall. Before going into my bedroom, I quietly knock on and then open the door to Mom and Dean's room. The empty bed is unmade, and the sheets are crumpled. Even the pillowcases repulse me with their yellow saliva stains. I wrinkle my nose at the smell of stale smoke and sweat that hangs in the air like a bad dream, as I close the door behind me.

Then there's Charlie's room. I force myself to pass by it without a glance. I know I'll never have the guts to leave with Nan if I open the door and see his Spiderman duvet cover or the posters of Toronto Raptor Rudy Gay that we plastered on the wall beside his bed. I need to move forward, even though it breaks my heart. Hopefully, Nan can find a way for Charlie to live with us, even though her apartment is really tiny.

I walk into my room. The silence consumes me. Everything is exactly as I left it, including the half-full glass of Coke on my dresser. The ghost of a watermark surrounds it.

I open my dresser drawer and half-heartedly throw a few pairs of underwear and socks into a large, tattered gym bag.

And that's when it hits me. Trixie. The house seems too empty because it is. It's completely empty. Trixie isn't here.

Heart thrumming, I race back to the living room. Nan is sitting on the couch, flipping through an old *People* magazine she must've fished out of the dusty magazine rack beside the TV. I stare for a moment at the beaming faces of Angelina Jolie and Brad Pitt.

"Where's Trixie?" I ask breathlessly. We passed her empty bed in the hallway when we first came in, and I hadn't thought about it until now. Sometimes it takes her a few minutes to wake up and make her way from one of the bedrooms to greet me, which is why I wasn't concerned at first.

But now it's clear she's not here.

Nan puts down her magazine. "Is she in one of the bedrooms?" she asks, her voice as calm as a morning ocean.

I'm the complete opposite. The feeling of panic is back. It's clawing at my throat, making me dizzy with fear. I stare wide-eyed at Nan.

"She's definitely not here. She's gone." Anxiety washes over me. I'm drowning with fear. "What if he's hurt her, or killed her just to get back at me? What if they stuck her outside, and she's freezing to death in a snow-bank somewhere? Or maybe Mom got rid of her to wipe away any memory of me because Trixie is really my dog since..." I pause to catch my breath. The memory of Trixie curled up beside Dad on the couch makes my words stick in my throat. "Since...well, you know."

Nan folds her hands together. "Since your daddy died?" she says softly. I wish I'd kept my big mouth shut. Nan hardly ever mentions Dad.

The front door opens, and my heart freezes. I notice Nan tense up as well. She clears her throat and dabs at her eyes.

"Let me take care of this, Lizzie," she says, straightening her shoulders. The look in her eyes means business. "Stop your worrying, and go pack your things."

I turn and start walking back to my room, my stomach twisting nervously. And that's when I hear Charlie.

Chapter Eight

"Lizzie! Nan!" Charlie squeals as he reaches the top of the staircase.

I turn and see him, Mom and Trixie. Relief floods through me. Trixie's okay. Mom bends to unclip the leash from her collar. As soon as she's freed, Trixie heads toward me with her tail wagging and Charlie beside her.

Mom straightens and stares at me like I've grown a third eye. That's when Nan steps forward. An uncomfortable energy fills the air.

"Hello, Kimi," she says. "We need to talk."

Mom looks at Nan. "Doreen, anything you have to say to me can be said in front of my children," she says flatly.

Nan glances my way, ignoring Mom's comment. "Lizzie, go to your room and gather your things. Charlie, you help your sister. We'll visit a bit as soon as your sister's done packing."

Charlie looks at me questioningly. "Packing?"

"Come on," I say, ignoring his question as I sweep Trixie up into my arms. "You can tell me what happened in school today."

Charlie's eyes darken with concern as he looks from Nan to me, but he follows me to my room without a word.

If there's one thing Charlie hates, it's any kind of conflict.

I shut the door and put Trixie down on my bed. Charlie sits beside her and watches me with wide, sad eyes as I sort through my closet. It's not like I've got a ton of clothes to choose from, but having to decide what I want to bring to Nan's suddenly becomes as difficult as brain surgery. With each top and pair of jeans I put into my backpack, my decision to leave becomes more real.

"You went to Nan's last night?" Charlie finally asks, biting his bottom lip nervously. He pauses, struggling to get out the questions he is so desperate to ask. "Why didn't you take me? Is it because I broke her Jesus plate?"

My heart twists into a painful knot. I kneel down in front of Charlie and throw my arms around him. He smells like freshly cut grass and baby shampoo mixed together.

"You still remember that?" I whisper into his hair. "Nan doesn't care that the plate was broken, buddy. She told you she didn't care when it happened."

Last time we were at Nan's together, Charlie stumbled and knocked into a bookshelf in the living room. Unfortunately, a hand-painted plate with the face of Jesus on it that was sitting on the top shelf couldn't survive the knock. It teetered drunkenly for a moment before crashing to the floor and shattering into what seemed like a thousand pieces. A shard skittered across the tile flooring and came to a rest at my feet. One of Jesus's big brown eyes stared up at me from the slice of plate. For nearly an hour Charlie sobbed, salty tears rolling down his cheeks. Nothing Nan and I did or said could console him. He knew, as we all did, just how much that plate had meant to her. She and Grandpa had brought it with them when they emigrated from

St. Lucia to Canada. It had been a gift from Nan's mother.

"Why are you leaving?" Charlie asks, pushing me away so he can look me in the eye. "I don't want you to go to Nan's."

I chew on my lip, unsure how to answer. It breaks my heart to hear the sadness in my brother's voice. Not only that, but I can detect his underlying fear. Though he's much younger than me, I'm not going to treat Charlie like he's stupid. He knows what a bastard Dean can be.

"I don't really want to go either," I say. "But I can't be around Dean anymore." I pause. How am I supposed to explain to Charlie what happened? "He's getting to be just too mean to me," I finally say.

Tears shine in Charlie's eyes. "But you can't leave." His face scrunches into an intense frown. "You're the only one who always makes sure things are okay here."

My blood freezes. Charlie's right. If I leave, things will definitely be more uncertain for him and Trixie. But I simply can't stay. Not after what happened. I get up and start to pack again, trying to think of a way to change the conversation. Somehow I need to make Charlie feel like things will be all right, that he only needs to hang on for a little while until I can figure out a solution with Nan.

"This is our home. He needs to go," Charlie says, interrupting my thoughts. His voice is cold. I've never heard him sound so full of hate. "I'm going to phone the police on Dean. They'll take him away, and then you can stay."

"No, you're not," I reply. "Do you know what the police will do if they find out that Dean hits me and Mom lets him? They'll take you and me away from here. They'll put us into foster homes. We could be split up forever. And Trixie will end up at the Humane Society—or worse."

Fear flashes across Charlie's face as he glances at Trixie, but his fists remain tightly clenched. Rage radiates off him in waves.

I'm not used to seeing my brother angry. Charlie's not a fighter. Until just a year or so ago, he'd hide under the kitchen table whenever Dean was being a drunken asshole, or when Dean and Mom would have their knockdown, epic arguments. Now Charlie's perched on the edge of my bed, shaking like a volcano about to blow. I guess we all have our breaking point.

I feel helpless. There's nothing I can say or do to make things better, so I resume packing in silence. With each piece of clothing I throw into my gym bag, I can't help but wonder if Charlie will end up hating me when I leave with Nan tonight. Maybe he'll think my words are all just lies and that I care only about myself, not him or Trixie. I wish I could explain everything more fully, but there's no way I want him to find out what happened with Dean. Just thinking about it makes my cheeks hot with shame.

"Are you mad at me?" Charlie asks, breaking the silence.

"Of course not. I'm more afraid that you're angry with me," I say with a halfhearted smile. "Everything will work out, you'll see. I just need a bit of time to figure everything out."

Charlie nods and reaches over to pet Trixie. "I'll take care of her," he says. "And don't worry, Lizzie, I won't phone the police, no matter what. I promise."

I watch my brother for a few moments as he continues to pet Trixie and whispers in her ear. Though his promise should reassure me, there's something in the tone of his voice that sends shivers through my blood.

Chapter Nine

"We really discourage students from transferring midway through the year like this," Ms. Smitherman says as she crosses her thin arms across her chest and leans back in her leather desk chair. The skin on her forearms is thin and folds like crepe paper across her sky-blue cashmere sweater. I look away and out the window at the snow twirling in the cold wind outside.

"Lizzie and I realize this isn't an ideal situation," Nan says. "However, due to a family emergency, her mother granted me temporary custody." She slides the lawyer's envelope across the desk toward Ms. Smitherman. "I have Lizzie's last report card in there as well. You'll see her grade-point average is very high."

Ms. Smitherman nods. "We'll try as much as we can to match your courses so you don't lose credits. In the meantime, you're welcome to pop into a few classes after sorting out your timetable with the guidance department. With only a few weeks left until Christmas, you'll really be starting in the new year. However, you're welcome to drop in on a few classes and get to know some of our teachers and students."

"That sounds good. I guess. I don't know," I say. The words stumble from my mouth. This feels surreal. Am I really transferring, leaving my school, Charlie and Trixie? Everything's changing so fast.

Ms. Smitherman stands and extends a veiny hand toward me. "Well, welcome to Mary Ann Shadd Secondary." Her nails are polished bright red, and a massive diamond ring sits heavily on one of her twiglike fingers. I gently touch her hand, afraid to shake it with any amount of force in case it snaps off like a bad Halloween joke.

"We appreciate you helping us like this," Nan says, standing and smoothing down the front of her black trousers. "And I'd love to see Lizzie involved in extracurricular activities while she's here at Mary Ann Shadd. She's a talented singer."

I stare at Nan, my body numb with shock. Why would she tell this Ms. Smitherman, someone who is pretty much a complete stranger, about something so personal? And what Nan doesn't know is that I've sung less and less since Dean moved in with us.

Ms. Smitherman smiles widely at me. Her teeth are Chicklet white. "We've got a fabulous drama club that puts on a show every year. In fact, we're only a week away from auditions." She sees the uninterested look on my face and raises an eyebrow at me. "This year's production is the *Wizard of Oz*, next year we will be doing *West Side Story*."

"Sorry, never heard of it," I say with as much politeness as I can manage. More than anything, I want to get out of this stuffy office. I wish Nan would just let me get my timetable and leave. Last night I only slept about three hours because I couldn't stop worrying about Charlie and Trixie. It probably didn't help that I was constantly checking my emails and text messages, hoping there'd be something from Fahad. My upper lids are lead shutters. I feel like a zombie.

Nan's eyes widen, and then she and Ms. Smitherman begin to howl with laughter. Annoyance bubbles up in me. I don't like being the butt of people's inside jokes, but I don't dare show Nan my feelings.

"Well, we need to change that," she finally says, catching her breath. "*West Side Story* was a groundbreaking Broadway show. And the movie was one of your daddy's favorites when he was your age."

My heart twists painfully at this bit of information. It's hard to think of Dad ever being my age. I'm sure he never imagined he'd die before the age of thirty when he was sitting watching *West Side Story* with Nan and Granddad.

Ms. Smitherman walks with us to the front of the office, where I'm handed my timetable by a stressed-looking secretary with frizzy red hair. Ms. Smitherman shakes Nan's hand.

"It was wonderful to meet both of you. I do hope to see Lizzie at least give the drama club a go." Her gaze falls on me. "The arts can be very cathartic, you know."

My upper eyelids are like sandbags—they're heavy and hard to keep open. I can barely see straight, let alone figure out what Ms. Smitherman is talking about.

"Healing, Lizzie," she says, clearly noting my confusion. "Something that is cathartic means it is very healing. Do consider popping in and at least meeting Ms. Philips. She's the head of the drama department and is very passionate about the club."

"Oh. Okay, I'll think about it," I reply, nodding in agreement just to end the conversation. My phone buzzes a text alert from deep inside the pocket of my leather jacket, causing my heart to leap. Could it be Fahad? Maybe he's realized that I didn't intend to create problems for him when I called the other night. Maybe he misses me and wants to apologize for breaking up with me the way he did.

Nan will kill me if I pull out my cell right now. She's big on good manners when it comes to cell phones. Another of her big pet peeves is when people answer their phones, or have them pulled out at all, in restaurants.

"Sorry, but I really need to go to the bathroom," I say. I'm interrupting Ms. Smitherman's and Nan's goodbyes, but I can't wait any longer to check the message.

Ms. Smitherman smiles. "The closest student bathroom is just down the hall to the left."

It takes all my willpower to make it down the hall and into a stall before pulling out my phone.

Sitting down on the closed toilet seat, I key in my security PIN. My heart sinks as soon as the text appears. It's not Fahad. In fact, the number is not even from my contacts list.

I read the message.

Lizzie, do you miss me? I miss you coz theres no one to play X-Box with. Im skared. Mom and dean fighted really bad last nite. Trixie was with me and peed in the bed coz no one took her for a walk. I told Mom it was me but she was mad. This is Charlie. Your brother.

The air is sucked out of me. I'm dizzy with emotion. I shouldn't have left Charlie and Trixie there alone. What was I thinking?

Charlie, of course I miss you! Wish I could've been there last night. Did anyone walk Trixie this morning? What phone are you using to text me? Love you. x Lizzie

I wipe my nose with the back of my hand. Charlie doesn't have a phone.

He must be texting me on a friend's phone, so I don't want to write too much. Other people don't need to know our business.

This is my phone. I tradid sum stuff for it. Sum of my games coz I need to be able to talk to you i miss you.

I call the number. Charlie answers after half a ring.

"Hello?" He sounds breathless. His voice is barely more than a whisper.

"Charlie, is everything okay? Mom still angry?"

"No…I don't know. She hasn't gotten out of bed yet." He's still whispering. "I can't really talk right now."

My heart begins to thunder in my ears. An uneasy feeling spreads through my insides like an ink stain. "Are you in class?"

Silence. Though it's only for a few seconds, Charlie's inability to answer tells me all I need to know.

"Are you at school? What's going on?" I ask.

"Everything's okay," he finally says. "It's just…can I call you later?"

"Later when?" I ask. Something's not right. He's not telling me the truth.

"Later today…maybe? For sure, tomorrow at school."

A sense of urgency sweeps over me. "What's going on, Charlie?"

The bad feeling is spreading deeper within me. Something's really not right. I glance at my watch. It's nearly 10:00 AM.

"You need to wake Mom up. You shouldn't be missing school. Have you eaten? Has Trixie had any food?"

"There's no food for Trixie. The bag was empty except for a couple of kibbles," Charlie whispers. "So I fed her hot dogs this morning."

Mom will freak when she finds food missing from the fridge, but I'm more worried about the fact that Trixie has no food. And that no one is walking her.

"I think I hear Mom," Charlie says. "I have to go. Lizzie?"

"Yeah?"

"Dean told Mom he's taking Trixie to the Humane Society today. I think that's why she's still in bed. He said that at the end of their big fight last night. She's really sad." His voice trembles with emotion.

I feel like I've just been slapped by a bag full of bricks. My heart plummets to my feet.

"What? Where's Dean now?" I'm not even going to bother asking Charlie if he thinks Dean is being serious. I know he's a big enough asshole to mean what he says. And deep down I also know there's little to no chance he'll pay the fifty-dollar fee to give an animal over to the Humane Society. Trixie's in real danger.

"I'm coming up there to get her as soon as I can," I say. "Don't let him take her out of the house, okay? I'll text or ring you when I'm close. You just need to bring her outside and around back. I'll wait behind the row of bushes for you."

"Okay," Charlie says. "Get here fast, Lizzie. Dean said he'd be back before lunch."

"Don't worry," I say. "It's going to be okay. I'll get there in time. Love you, buddy." I hang up the phone and stare at an angry smear of graffiti on the back of the toilet-stall door. It feels like someone's punched me in the gut and left me gasping for oxygen.

I have no idea how I'm going to save Trixie, but I'm willing to die trying.

Chapter Ten

"You know how I feel. No animals in the house," Nan says.

We're leaving the school, milky clouds of vapor spilling out of our mouths and noses with every breath. It's freezing. Trixie won't be able to last long outside in this weather. She's too little and thin. It's already eleven fifteen. Time's running out. I'm going to have to text Charlie soon to put her outside or else take the chance that Dean is just making a false threat. But after what happened the other night, my guess is that his threats are anything but empty.

"I'm sorry your mother continues to allow that man to rule her life and take precedence over her children, Lizzie. However, there's no changing my mind. My firm belief is that animals should be kept in the yard, not in the home."

"But you don't have a yard," I protest. I'm know I'm walking on thin ice. Questioning Nan is not something I'd normally do unless I wanted to walk around headless, but this situation is desperate. Trixie's life depends on me.

"I know this is difficult for you," Nan says. Her black leather boots click rhythmically on the sidewalk. I find myself having to put in effort just to keep up. "But perhaps Trixie being surrendered to the Humane Society is not the worst thing in the world. It could give her the chance to be adopted by a family that can properly care for her and look after her needs as she gets older. And God knows we could all use that."

I nod. Nan has a point, but I'm not willing to give Trixie up that easily. "The thing is, I don't believe Dean will take her to the Humane Society. He'd never pay to have them take her." I pause for a moment. "And she helped Dad so much when he was sick. She stuck by his side nearly every moment, day and night."

There's a quick intake of breath from Nan. "All the more reason she deserves a better home than the one Dean and your mother are giving her. A home with love, rather than one run by two drunks." There's a hardness to her voice and a fiery look in her eyes that tell me our conversation needs to end. So, even though I know she must realize Dean won't try to find Trixie a loving home, I'm not going to push it further.

In fact, I don't think I've ever seen her look this angry. And that's when I realize Mom's decisions over the last few years haven't just affected Charlie and me. The things she's done—and neglected to do—have impacted Nan and others who loved Dad and were close to our family. It makes me think about people like the Andersons. They were really good friends with Mom and Dad. We'd go over there on a Saturday night at least once a month for dinner. Afterward, while the adults sat and finished off bottles of wine, Charlie and I would hang out with their twins. Jermaine and Aleysha were a couple of years younger than me, but I didn't mind because we'd mostly play video games or watch movies.

The Andersons came over often when Dad was sick. Every visit, they brought

Tupperware containers full of green banana and saltfish (Dad's favorite) and homemade soups for when his chemotherapy made it difficult for him to keep food down. They came to the wake and the funeral and visited us often after Dad died. Then Mom started drinking a lot more and bringing home boyfriends who didn't have much in common with the Andersons. Eventually, after Dean came along, they visited us less and less, and we completely stopped going for dinner at their house.

I haven't thought of the Andersons in a long time. I wonder if they ever think of us, and how they feel about the way Mom ditched their friendship. Or maybe they were the ones who decided to step out of our lives. Either way, it is another sign of how much of our past Dean has managed to destroy.

"I'd like to go back to my old school today to say goodbye to a few friends and teachers," I tell Nan as we walk into the lobby of her apartment building. "Besides, I need to clear out my locker. I have loads of things in there like gym clothes and library books that need to be returned."

It's not a complete lie. All those things are in my locker. It's just I couldn't care less about going back to get them. And even if I did care, there's no way I'd chance going back to school and running into Fahad. I couldn't handle that.

Nan fumbles around in her chestnut-colored leather purse for her key. "I don't know why you'd want to go running up there today when it's as cold as bones outside." She fishes her key out of the purse and slides it into the apartment door's lock.

"I won't really have another chance to go," I say, walking inside with her. I don't bother taking off my shoes or coat. Every moment I'm not making my way uptown means Trixie's life is in greater danger. "So…I'll get going if that's okay. I'll be as fast as I can."

Nan nods. "Get all your things. Anything you need before starting at Mary Ann Shadd, let me know as soon as you return. We'll go pick up any bits and pieces you require this weekend so that you're ready to go on Monday."

I give her a quick hug and kiss on the cheek, which catches Nan completely off guard. She shoos me away with a wave of her hand and a roll of her eyes. *Affectionate* is definitely not a word I'd use to describe Nan, though I know she loves me more than anything and would risk her life without thinking to save mine. And I would do the same for her.

As soon as the door shuts behind me, I begin running down the hall as fast as I can.

Chapter Eleven

A doughy-looking, middle-aged man with a only few wisps of black hair on his head sits across from me on the streetcar. He's picking his nose and then wiping it along the steel-rimmed pane of the window, leaving a trail of snail-like slime. I try not to watch, but it's like a bad traffic accident where everyone slows down their cars to get a glimpse.

There's something both gross and hypnotizing about it. The crazy thing is, he's not even trying to hide what he's doing. Every once in a while he turns and smiles at other passengers, with his index finger so far up his nose you'd swear he was mining brains.

Eventually I turn away and stare out the window at the heavy traffic slowing the bus down. My phone buzzes from deep inside my jacket pocket. It's Charlie.

Lizzie—Dean will be back soon. Puting Trixie out side with her blankit tyed behind the bushes by parking lot.

The streetcar is pulling into the subway station. I have only a few seconds to text Charlie back. How can I tell him I'm still a subway ride away? I'm going to have to run the entire distance from the station home.

Take my duvet off the bed. Wrap her in it. Hopefully no one will notice.

Be there soon, buddy. Will text you when I've got her.

I rush from the streetcar and into the crowded subway station. Flashing my card at the ticket seller, I take the stairs two at a time down to the platform. The monitor hanging from the ceiling informs me that the next train is in five minutes. My heart sinks. So much can happen in just five minutes. Someone could discover Trixie and take her or mistake the duvet as something that needs to be thrown in the trash. Nervous beads of sweat erupt on my forehead.

My phone vibrates again. I'm surprised to be able to receive a signal down here. It's Charlie. My heart sinks as I read his message.

Dean home. Trixie out side. She was crying bad when I left her. Afrade Dean will go out and here her. He is look for her now. Starting to yell. Get here fast. Love Charlie.

The train approaches the platform with a screech. Chimes sound and people pour out, many of them carrying bags full of Christmas shopping. I rush forward and onto the train. My heart is thumping so loudly in my chest I'm sure everyone around me can hear it.

Dad, if you're up there and can help at all, please let me get to Trixie on time. Please.

By the time we reach the stop closest to home, more than twenty-five minutes have passed since Charlie's last text. I push my way to the front of the doors and past several other passengers.

"Wait your turn," an elderly woman carrying a tiny dog in her arms snaps at me.

I turn back for a second. The little dog makes me think of Trixie, and I immediately feel bad.

"Sorry," I reply.

Eyes narrowed, the woman sticks a bony middle finger at me in response and clutches her dog closer to her chest.

That's enough for me to not care at all about the passengers I rush by on the escalator. They can swear at me all they want. The only thing on my mind now is Trixie.

The cold air hits me like a slap as I slam through the glass doors at the entrance of the station. I begin to run, pacing myself as much as possible. If I can keep running like this, I'll reach Trixie in less than five minutes.

My lungs are liquid fire, and my shoes don't give me any grip on the slippery sidewalk. I slip once and crash down to the sidewalk. I hold out my hand to soften my fall, and the palm of my left mitten shreds like cheese on the frozen concrete. But I don't slow down. By the time I reach the corner of our street,

I'm tired and gulping at the air like a fish out of water.

My phone vibrates in my pocket. I pull off the mitten on my right hand and take it out. My left hand is throbbing with pain.

Lizzie where are you? Dean is MAD. Hes yelling at mom. Thinks shes hidding trixie.

Two seconds away, buddy. Do you need me to come in?

I'm speed-walking toward our building when a wave of fear washes over me. What if Dean comes out and sees me? What if he comes out and finds Trixie before I do?

I pull my hood over my head, which makes me feel better, and cut across the parking lot toward the bushes. There are no leaves left on the spindly branches. I spot the flowers of my red-and-white duvet on the other side of the bushes and break into a jog.

"Trixie?" I say, keeping my voice low. The duvet moves slightly. I lean down, and that's when I hear soft whimpering.

I lift the edge of the duvet and peer inside. Trixie looks up at me, her tail wagging weakly. She whimpers again. That's when I notice she's shaking like a leaf in a thunderstorm.

"Hey, girl," I say, leaning in and rubbing her fur. "I'm here now. It's okay."

Trixie's tail thumps a little harder in response, and she tries to lift her head. I've got to get her out of the cold and get some food and water in her. I unzip my coat, scoop her up and place her inside my coat. Hopefully, my body heat will help stop the intense shivers she's having. Though I hate leaving my duvet laying in the snow like a piece of unwanted trash, there's no way I can take it back to Nan's. Not only would it be a nightmare to take on the subway, but Nan would know straight away that I didn't come up here to clear out my locker.

And that's when I realize two things: Charlie hasn't gotten back to me, and Nan's going to expect me to come home with at least some of my school stuff.

I zip up my jacket, using one arm to make sure Trixie is supported. She feels so light. How did I not notice she was becoming this thin? Her shivering hasn't stopped yet. I push that worry to the back of my mind as I text Charlie with one hand.

Charlie? Is everything okay? I can come in.

If I need to go into our place, I'll leave Trixie in the downstairs hall. I won't let Dean hurt her. Or let him hurt Charlie and Mom. He'll have to kill me first. Thing is, I'm not so sure he wouldn't.

My phone buzzes.

Dont come in. every thing okay. Dean will hurt you. trixie okay?

I've got Trixie. You call me if things aren't, okay? Promise? Call the police if you need to.

I bite nervously at my bottom lip while waiting for his reply.

I will call if things get wurse. Love you Lizzie.

Part of me feels like I should go in to be sure Charlie is safe, but I know Dean will probably calm down once he realizes Trixie is actually gone. After all, that's all he really wants. Trixie is a reminder of our old life with Dad, and now she's also a reminder of me. Plus, feeding her means less money for booze, and that must drive Dean nuts.

I begin to walk back to the subway. I've only got about fifteen dollars left of the money I took from Dean. It should be enough to get some food for Trixie. Thing is, I need to find a safe place for her to stay until I can figure out a more permanent solution.

I peek inside my jacket, and Trixie looks up at me with her soulful brown eyes. Her tail wags against my side.

"It's going to be okay, girl," I say. "I promise."

She reaches up and gives me a moist lick on the cheek. It feels almost like she understands what I'm trying to do for her.

Thing is, more and more I can't get rid of the bad feeling spreading through my insides like water from a slow-leaking tap. I'm promising things will be okay for those I love when I don't even believe it myself anymore.

Chapter Twelve

"Who is it?" The voice on the other side of the door is sharp and suspicious. Trixie wiggles around uncomfortably in my jacket. It's been a long ride to get back down here, including a stop at No Frills to pick up some dog food. She seems to be gaining a bit more energy, which makes me happy.

"Maie? It's me. Lizzie." I don't want to be too loud out here in the hall. I'm worried about Nan hearing me. "Can I come in?"

I wait as the locks on the door click, and it swings open. Maie wheels out of the way so that I can walk in.

She's wearing a bright red shawl over flowing flowered trousers, and her hair is pulled back into a neat bun.

"I had my home-care nurse in today," she explains with a broad smile and a wink. "I always make sure I pick something special out for her to help me get into. It's good to see you, Lizzie. How are you settling in with Rosie?"

"Nan's been great. She helped me get into school and everything." I pause, rocking back and forth on my feet. Maie's my only chance. More important, she's Trixie's last chance.

Maie gestures toward the sofa. "Park yourself, girl! You're making me nervous. What's wrong?"

"I need your help," I say, sitting down and unzipping my jacket. Trixie barely moves, so I lift her up gingerly for Maie to see.

Maie's eyes widen. "Where did you get that precious toy poodle from?" She wheels closer, and Chester barks excitedly as Trixie comes into view. "Hush, Chester," she says. "This little one doesn't look well, Lizzie. She yours?"

I nod, tears springing to my eyes. My lips tremble as I try to speak. "Nan won't let me keep her in the apartment. But I had to take her. She wasn't being cared for properly where she was." My voice cracks with emotion.

Maie places a plump hand on my arm. Her skin is powder smooth. "It's okay," she says, leaning over and giving

Trixie a gentle pat on the head. Trixie licks her in return.

"Your nan grew up in the countryside in the West Indies. Animals weren't pets. You can understand that, right?"

I nod, unable to speak. Tears are flowing down my face now.

"I don't want to give her to a shelter." Tears and snot mingle on my upper lip. "But I have no one to take her. She stayed with my dad the entire time he was sick. Left his side only to eat and go to the bathroom."

Maie reaches over and scratches Trixie behind her ears. "Is that right, good girl?" she whispers, her voice gentle. Trixie leans her face into Maie's hand.

"I hate to ask, but could you keep her for a bit? Just until I can figure something else out?"

Maie stops petting Trixie and sits back heavily in her chair. "Lizzie, I'd love to take her, but…"

"Please," I whisper, not fully trusting my voice. "Really bad things are happening at home right now. That's why I left in the middle of the night to come here and live with Nan." Reaching inside my backpack, I pull out the bag of dry kibble and cans of wet dog food I bought at No Frills. "This is all I have for her right now, but I'm going to get a part-time job. That way Nan can take in my little brother, Charlie. And then I can give you money for Trixie."

Maie's eyes darken with concern. "I'm happy to care for Trixie as long as I possibly can," she says. "And I'm a damn fine nurse, but I'm not sure she won't be needing to see a vet. If that's the case, I can't afford to pay those bills, and neither can you."

I understand completely. If Trixie needs more care, I'll have to surrender her to a shelter. At this point, all I can do is hope.

"I know," I say. My nose begins to run as I place Trixie on Maie's couch. "Thank you so much. I'll come by every morning and night to walk her and Chester. I promise."

"You come by any time, but your schoolwork comes before walking the dogs. I can do that just fine with my four-wheeler," Maie says, passing me a pink tissue from a box on the coffee table. "I know there are secrets weighing you down, Lizzie. And I'm here when you're ready to share those. Does your nan know what's been going on at home?"

I shake my head. "No. I need to figure things out first before I tell her everything. It's pretty intense," I say, standing and zipping my jacket back up. "Speaking of Nan, I better get back to her. I'll come by tomorrow morning, okay?" Since it'll be Saturday, there'll be no worry about school. It's going to be hard to be away from Trixie even overnight though. I'm afraid she won't get better if I'm gone and she's left in a strange place.

As soon as I'm inside at Nan's, I kick off my shoes and walk into the living room. She's sitting in her favorite burgundy velvet chair, black-rimmed glasses perched on her nose, reading the newspaper. She insists on being old school when it comes to the newspaper and has it delivered in hard copy to her apartment door, even though it regularly gets stolen.

"That was quite a while," Nan says, folding the newspaper on her lap. "Everything work out?"

I twist my face into a frown. "Not really. You won't believe what happened. My lock was cut. All my stuff was cleared out of the locker."

"What?" Nan asks, her voice sharp with concern. She sits straight up.

"That's unacceptable. What do you mean your things are missing? Why would your lock be cut?"

My story has more holes in it than a slice of Swiss cheese. Nan's right. Why would my lock be randomly cut?

"I don't mean cut. Well, not exactly. A bunch of lockers were broken into. The school is looking into it...the locks may have been cut. I don't know. I guess they don't know...at least not yet." I'm rambling, so I sit down on the sofa. "It's not a huge deal. Just lost some library books and a smelly change of gym clothes."

Nan stares hard at me for a moment, and I get the feeling she wants to ask me more. Raising an eyebrow, she settles back into her chair. "Well, I doubt that kind of nonsense will be happening at your new school. I know you're not officially attending until the new year, but I think it would be good for you to go in on Monday and meet a few of the teachers, and maybe drop in on that drama club."

"Sure," I say, tucking my feet under me. "Oh, I ran into Maie in the lobby. She asked me if I could walk Chester in the mornings for the next while."

Nan's eyes darken. "She did? Did she say why?"

"No." I'm taken off guard by Nan's questions, but I shouldn't be. I'm digging myself deeper and deeper into a sticky web of lies. "She looked kind of tired to me. I guess she might just be feeling a bit off."

Nan nods. "I'd be grateful if you could do that for her," she says. "And if you need a break, I'll be happy to help you walk Chester. I sometimes look after him so she can go to bingo on a Saturday night."

My heart leaps into my chest. "That's okay. It'll be good for me to get up early and stuff." How would either Maie or I explain the sudden appearance of a second dog? And I certainly can't ask Maie to lie to Nan about Trixie. She's already doing so much for me.

"Well, how does chicken and rice with some greens sound for dinner?" Nan asks, folding her newspaper and placing it on the table beside her. I could be wrong, but she almost seems a bit sad.

"Great," I say, getting up so I can help her in the kitchen. "Can I ask you something?"

"I have a feeling you're going to even if I say no," Nan says with a laugh as she stands up.

"What did Mom say to you when we went over to get my stuff? About me being here? About what's been happening at home?" My stomach does a nervous flip-flop. Shame reddens my cheeks.

Nan looks hard at me. "Lizzie, your mother has a very serious issue with alcohol. What she has to say holds little water with me. It's the addiction talking, not her."

"But what did she say?" I feel like a little kid begging for a chocolate bar at the supermarket. Though I know Nan doesn't want to tell me, and that I should just let it go, I don't. Suddenly, nothing in the world matters more than finding out what was said when Mom and Nan talked the other day.

"Your mother thinks you're trying to seduce Dean. And because of that, she doesn't want you back in the house." Nan looks at me, her eyes wide with sadness. "Then I told her she was as mad as a dog with rabies, and that she needed to get herself together or else I'd be coming for Charlie as well."

Chapter Thirteen

Throughout dinner I try to push what Nan said out of my mind. After all, I should hardly be surprised. The night I left, Mom made it clear she believed Dean when he said I'd been hitting on him. But to not want me back at home? That hurts so deeply. Does she mean forever?

"Something wrong with my cooking?" Nan asks, watching me push the remaining rice and greens around on my plate.

I can't manage another bite. There's nothing wrong with the food—I just feel too nauseous to eat. Usually Nan wouldn't stand for waste, but I think she knows what's up. My heart feels like it's splintered inside my chest. Everything aches on a soul level.

After washing the dishes, I go to my room. It is actually a den the size of a walk-in closet. I want to check my messages in case Charlie's tried contacting me.

I sit down on the air mattress Nan bought for me to use as a bed. It's not as bad as it sounds. I've got a couple of warm blankets, and the mattress is surprisingly comfortable considering it's not much more than a big rectangular balloon.

I've got three new texts and two phone messages. I cross my fingers, hoping everything's okay with Charlie, and open my text messages.

As soon as I see who sent the messages, my blood runs cold, and my hands start to shake. None of them are from Charlie. They're from Fahad. All three messages. Taking a deep breath, I begin to read.

Baby girl, I'm sorry I blew you off like I did. Where have you gone to?

I just couldn't deal. My parents were on me like gum on a shoe. No excuses, felt I'd had nuff but can't leave my girl on her own.

Missing you. Give us another chance?

My fingers begin dialing before my brain can talk sense into me.

Fahad answers after just one ring.

"Hey, you," he says. "Let me just get to my bedroom to talk."

I don't say anything. Instead I wait, holding my breath. There was definite happiness in his voice when he answered the phone, which allows my body to relax for the first time since everything happened with Dean.

"Baby, where you been?" he asks. "Is everything okay?"

"I'm transferring to Mary Ann Shadd Secondary," I reply. "Mom doesn't want me living with her anymore." My voice trembles as I say the words out loud. I know Nan keeps telling me it's not Mom talking, just the alcohol and addiction, but I still have my doubts. Maybe Mom was looking for an excuse to get rid of me because Dean and I fought so much.

"What? That's all the way downtown," Fahad says. "What do you mean your mom doesn't want you at home? She kick you out?"

"I'm living with my nan in Regent Park. It's one of the closest secondary schools." I stop, not really wanting to get into the reasons behind Mom kicking me out. Thinking about it makes me feel like I've fallen down a dark hole. I don't want Fahad knowing too much, especially about what Dean did to me. What if he ended up believing it was my fault, just like Mom did? We'd have no chance of getting back together then.

"How are we gonna see each other?" he asks. "We'll only have the weekends. Does your nan know you've got a boyfriend?"

"No, because I didn't think I had a boyfriend anymore," I answer quietly. Of course, it's not something I would've told Nan anyhow. I have the feeling she'd think fifteen is too young to be dating and that I should be concentrating on school instead.

"Lizzie, I'm sorry I went off on you like that. I was stressed with exams and studying, and your call was the last straw. I just needed a break from all your drama."

"You realize I don't want this drama, right?" I say, trying to keep the hurt out of my voice. "It's not like this is the life I'd choose. I'd do anything to have my dad and my family the way it used to be."

"I didn't mean it like that, baby," Fahad says. "Listen, why don't I come down there this weekend? Is there a place we can meet alone? Somewhere warm?"

Having Fahad back in my life right now would mean so much. I don't want to say no to him, but I'm afraid that if Nan finds out I have a boyfriend, she might wonder if I am a bit of a slut like Mom says I am.

Suddenly, the perfect plan hits me. "I have an idea how we can be alone and hang out for a bit tomorrow night," I say. "But I'll need to get back to you in the morning. Okay?"

"Sounds good. Sweet dreams."

With that, Fahad ends our call. Though I should be feeling really good about getting back together, I get off the phone feeling nervous about seeing him again. How do I know he won't just turn around and not want me again?

Chapter Fourteen

The next morning I'm up with Nan. The sun has barely risen. Shuffling to the kitchen, I pour myself freshly made coffee from the pot and toast some multigrain bread. Feeling like a complete zombie, I sit down at the table to eat. I didn't sleep well last night, as I couldn't get Trixie's health, Charlie and the worry about what is going to happen with Fahad and me off my mind.

"Well, you're up early," Nan says with a smile. She is wide-eyed and so full of energy that I wonder if she's some kind of superhuman cyborg instead of a regular sixty-year-old.

"I've got to get to Maie's to take the dogs…I mean, Chester, for a walk." I stuff a piece of toast into my mouth and take a final swig of coffee.

"Go easy on the coffee, Lizzie," Nan says. "At your age, you shouldn't really be having any at all. Bad for the skin and the mind. Are you sure you don't want some company?"

"The walk will give me a chance to clear my head." I feel bad saying no to Nan's offer to join me. She's likely wondering why I don't want her to come along. "I'll be back shortly."

"Just be careful and watch your surroundings," Nan says, blowing on her tea. "The streets can still be alive at this time."

I run back and give her a kiss on the cheek. "Will do. Love you, Nan."

She shoos me away with her hand. "Go on. Stop getting all mushy on me."

With a laugh, I turn and head to Maie's place.

Maie answers the door on the fourth knock. She's in her housecoat and has a red-and-black-paisley bandanna wrapped around her head. Her appearance takes me by surprise. Dark circles line her eyes, and her skin is corpse white. She looks really sick.

"Come on in, Lizzie," she says weakly. "Do you want a coffee?"

"I hope I didn't wake you up," I say, taking a few steps inside. "Am I too early?"

At the sound of my voice, Trixie comes running from the kitchen. She barks excitedly. Relief washes over me. She looks much better than yesterday.

In fact, I swear her fur and eyes are shining in a way I haven't seen for a long time. I scoop her into my arms, and she bathes my face with ticklish kisses.

Maie coughs deeply. Her chest sounds like it's stuffed with glue. She shakes her head at me as she tries to regain her voice. "Not…not too early at all. I've been up for hours. Hard to sleep last night, and I wanted to keep your sweet Trixie company."

"Thanks so much. She looks great. I think you've had a really healing effect," I say, clipping Trixie's leash onto her collar.

Maie reaches down to unclip Chester from her scooter. "My love, I truly wish I had the power to heal. Have a lovely walk. Are you going to be warm enough out there?" Her eyes scan my torn jeans and sneakers.

"Yeah," I say. "The cold doesn't really bother me."

Maie shakes her head and laughs. It's a deep, raspy laugh. "You young ones. I'm going to get myself more present-able while you're all out." She laughs again, except this time her laughter is tinged with sadness.

I suddenly remember my plans with Fahad. "Nan said you like to go to bingo. If she went with you tonight, would you go? I'd be happy to stay here and look after the dogs."

The sagging corners of Maie's mouth slowly turn up into a smile. "I just might be able to find a spare couple of dollars and my lucky dolls to do that. Thank you, Lizzie. If Rosie doesn't mind helping me get there and back, I'd love to go."

Her voice is full of gratitude, which immediately makes me feel like a jerk. After all, I'm mainly offering to watch the dogs so that I can have Fahad over. And I'm not even telling Maie that I'm inviting a stranger into her home.

Nan would take my head and bounce it into next week if she knew. I wonder if I should just tell Fahad to come and meet me at Tim Hortons. Thing is, I want to see him somewhere more private if I can.

I take Chester's and Trixie's leashes and head out. Maie was right. It's cold outside, and it feels like I'm snorting dry ice every time I breathe in. Both Trixie and Chester are pretty small dogs, so I figure we'll all feel better if I keep the walk short.

We turn down the street, past rows of new townhouses. The ones that people with money bought are slightly nicer than the ones on the opposite side of the street. Those ones, which are lived in by real Regent Park residents, don't have balconies with expensive barbecues, one-car garages or fancy alarm systems. I lead the dogs toward a large park by what turns out to be an aquatic center. One side of the building is almost entirely windows, and I can see what looks like a water aerobics class for older people going on. For some reason, this makes me sad. I sit down on a bench and begin to cry.

The tears won't stop coming. I take in big gulps of icy air and try to suffocate my sobs. It's too much. I can't do this. Images and feelings from the other night with Dean come flooding back. I'm confused. I feel like a whore. Trixie begins to whimper.

"Hey, are you okay?" a soft voice asks.

I look up and am startled to see a woman directly in front of me. Her dark hair is slightly messy, and mascara smudges the skin under her deep-brown eyes. My eyes travel over her black booty shorts, knee-high stiletto boots and her slightly dirty, silver metallic jacket. She looks exhausted.

"Aren't you cold?" I ask, drawing Trixie and Chester closer to me.

The woman laughs. It's a nice laugh, kind of musical and full of joy. "Pretty girl, don't worry about me. You're the one out here crying like your heart's being torn apart by a pack of wild dogs."

"I'm okay," I say. "Just not feeling great about my life and who I am at the moment. Thanks for asking though." And I mean it. This woman took the time to stop and make sure I'm all right even though I'm a total stranger.

She frowns. "Don't let that feeling continue. You're a pretty girl. Bet you have people who care about you and love you."

Generally, I would've gotten up at this point and walked away. But something about this woman makes me stay.

"My mom kicked me out. Her boyfriend...he..." I pause, my voice catching in my throat. "He abuses me. And I don't even know if my boyfriend is actually my boyfriend anymore."

Tears roll down my cheeks, quickly turning into little rivers of salty ice.

Sadness fills the woman's eyes. "I understand—believe me, I do. But I didn't ask you that. I asked who loves you and cares about you." She runs her hand through her hair, and I notice her skyscraper-sized, cherry-red nails.

"My nan does," I reply, thinking about how she took me in without question when I showed up. "And her best friend, Maie, cares for me as well."

"See, all you need is two people in this world to love you." She's shivering now, moving back and forth to warm herself.

"You need to get inside," I say. "It's too cold out. I'm going to have to head back to my nan's as well."

"What I need is a cigarette and a coffee," the woman says, her voice thick with sadness again. "Well, it was nice meeting you…"

"Elizabeth…Lizzie. My name is Lizzie," I say, reaching out to shake her hand. That's when I notice how thin her wrist is and see the white scars running up and down her coffee-colored skin. She sees me looking and pulls down the sleeve of her coat.

"It was wonderful meeting you, Lizzie," she says, smiling widely at me. "Take care of yourself and have a Merry Christmas."

"You too," I say, getting up and heading back the way that I came. Suddenly I realize I didn't get her name.

"Hey, I don't know your name." Clouds of white vapor stream into the air with each word. "And how come two people? Why don't you need just one person to love you?"

She stops and turns around. "You need someone in this world to love you like your nan does, but, more important, you need to love yourself, Lizzie.

Don't end up like me, not loving yourself enough to stop selling your body
to people who don't care if you live or
die. And it's Angel. My name is Angel."
With that she turns on her massive heels
and unsteadily makes her way along the
sidewalk toward Dundas Street.

Chapter Fifteen

I meet Fahad at the corner of Parliament and Carlton at six o'clock. As soon as he steps off the streetcar, I can't help smiling. He walks over and gives me a massive hug. I hold him close, breathing in the familiar scent of his cologne mingled with mint gum.

"I missed you so much," I say. Trixie

and Chester are both with me, and Fahad bends down to pet them.

"You didn't say you brought Trixie along with you," he says with a frown. "This is for real, isn't it?"

I nod as we begin to walk. "Yeah, it's for real," I reply, stopping to untangle the dogs' leashes.

A light snow begins to fall, giving the crowded street a false feeling of calm. Colored lights adorn the lampposts and shop windows. I realize there are only two weeks left until Christmas and can't imagine Charlie being on his own, without me, that morning. Even though we didn't get much in the way of presents, we always got each other something small, and Mom usually got us each something we wanted.

I check my watch. Nan and Maie were leaving at six, so I figure we're pretty safe to head back.

"We can go to my friend Maie's place," I say. "Chester's her dog."

"Sounds good." Fahad pulls his hood farther down over his forehead and narrows his eyes against the falling snow. "Are you really not coming back to Roseview? To the hood?"

"I don't really know," I say, swiping the fob against the apartment's front-door keypad. "Everything is really screwed-up right now. I'm not going home anytime soon. And I definitely won't go back if Dean is still there."

"Too bad we couldn't just make him disappear," Fahad says. "I'd love to get my hands on that guy in a dark alley. Just a few minutes somewhere private. He'd never bother you again."

Tears spring to my eyes. We're in the elevator, and so even though I turn my head away, my reflection in the mirrored walls gives me away.

"Hey, baby," Fahad says, drawing me close. "Why are you crying?"

Because I feel like a whore, I want to say. Angel's words come back to me. She's right. I've hated myself since that night with Dean. I still hate him, but now I hate myself just as much.

"I need to talk to my nan," I say. "And I need to go to the police." My hands are shaking uncontrollably. What if the police don't believe me? What if Nan doesn't? And I don't want to tell Fahad what Dean did to me. I'm afraid he'll never want to stay with me if I do.

But this is the one chance I have to make Dean disappear. I need to tell people about him raping me.

We step off the elevator and Fahad hugs me. "Okay, we'll talk to your nan together when she gets home." He bends down to kiss me.

I freeze. "No, don't. I can't." The shaking is getting worse. Tiny stars dance across my vision, and my knees give way. I slump against the wall. The dogs begin to bark.

Fahad leans down beside me. "Lizzie, what's going on with you? What's happened?"

He doesn't want drama. And I don't blame him. What sixteen-year-old guy needs this? I don't want drama either, but if I don't deal with this, it's going to kill me. Maybe it will kill me anyhow. I don't know.

"I have to see Nan now. It can't wait."

He wraps his arm around me. "Okay, we'll find her, baby. It's okay. I'm sorry I left."

An apartment door across the hall opens up. A man with a red, pudding-like face sticks his head out. He's wearing a white undershirt, and black, spiky hairs stick out the top of it like spider's legs.

"Keep it down, will ya?" he shouts. "Find yourselves a motel room if you need to." He slams the door shut.

We both begin to laugh. I feel like I'm walking a tightrope and am one fall away from crazy.

Fahad helps me up. "Where's your nan at?" he asks, bending down to give Chester and Trixie some reassuring pats.

"She's at bingo with Maie at the community center," I say. "It's only a few blocks away from here."

My phone begins to ring. It's Charlie.

"Hey, buddy," I say, trying to make my voice as cheery as possible. I don't want him to know I've been upset.

"Lizzie?" Charlie's voice is high-pitched and thick with panic. "Lizzie, you need to come home."

"What's going on?" My heart begins to thump in my ears. "Charlie?" There's noise in the background, a loud banging.

"The phone. I stole it from my teacher, and someone ratted me out, so the school called about an hour ago. And Dean's drunk and really mad, and I need you to come…quick, Lizzie. He's hurting Mom because she's trying to keep him from hurting me." He's almost screaming the words now. Fahad's eyes widen. Charlie's so loud, he can hear it all.

"Where are you now?" I ask.

"I'm in the bathroom," Charlie says. The banging is getting louder. "He's trying to get in. I don't know what he's done to Mom. I can't hear her anymore." He begins to cry.

"Jesus, it's like *The Shining*," Fahad says. "That mother…"

"Charlie, listen to me. Phone the police now. Get off and phone 9-1-1.

I'm on my way." I'm unlocking Maie's door and leading the dogs inside.

"*We're* on our way," Fahad says as I get off my phone and lock the apartment door. The dogs bark frantically at me from the other side. They know something's wrong.

Fahad's already on his phone. "Police," he says as we rush into the elevator. "Yes, I'd like to report an assault involving a young child." He looks over at me. "We need to get to a bank machine. I'll get money for a taxi."

Chapter Sixteen

We don't speak until we're in the taxi.
It's like we're robots on a mission.
All I can think about is Charlie. I try
to call him back, but the line is busy.
I assume he's being kept on the phone
by the police, and I only have a couple
of bars left on my phone. I write down
the phone number Charlie's on just in

case my phone dies. If it does we can still try to contact him on Fahad's phone.

"I'm so sorry, Lizzie, I didn't know things had gotten so bad," Fahad says, putting his arm around me.

I don't say anything, because he really did bail when it was pretty clear things were getting worse for me at home. I'd never called him in the middle of the night before that one time. Sometimes I'd Facebooked him, but I'd never phoned. I am grateful he's here right now, but I'm not going to say it's okay just so he can feel better.

"I need to call Nan," I say. "Can I use your phone?"

Fahad nods and hands it to me. Then he turns to the window and looks out at the thick traffic. We're moving at a snail's pace.

Nan answers after two rings. It's hard to hear her over the background noise.

"Nan, I need you to come to Mom's. Things are really bad. Fahad and I are heading up there in a taxi right now."

"What do you mean things are bad? What exactly is going on?" Nan asks. "Who's Fahad?"

"He's my boyfriend." Fahad grabs my hand and gives it a squeeze. "Charlie called me a few minutes ago. He took his teacher's phone the other day, and I guess the school called today to tell Mom. Dean's on a rampage. He's trying to hurt Charlie."

"Listen to me, Lizzie. You are not to go in there without the police. Promise?" Nan says. "It's too dangerous. I'm on my way. I just need to take Maie home first."

"Okay," I say. Nan must know I won't wait for the police. And they better be there by now. It's already been ten minutes since I told Charlie to call 9-1-1. Our taxi is still creeping up the

Don Valley Parkway. It will take us nearly an hour to get there at this speed.

We sit in silence for a few minutes, and I watch the taximeter climb. It's already at thirty-five dollars. I didn't notice how much money Fahad got out, and I feel terrible that it's going to cost him so much.

"Is there a faster way to get there?" Fahad finally asks the driver. Beads of sweat stand out on his forehead. The taxi interior is stuffy, and I wipe condensation off the window. The snow is getting worse, which isn't helping the traffic.

"Want me to grow wings?" the driver growls at Fahad. "I'm not risking my life so you can arrive a few minutes sooner at some Saturday-night party to drink your face off."

"I don't drink," Fahad replies through gritted teeth. "It's haram."

The driver shrugs his shoulders. "Potato, po-tat-o. I'm still not going to bust my neck for you two."

Fahad sits back heavily in his seat and rolls his eyes. "Figures we get the only non-Muslim cab driver in Toronto."

I try Charlie several more times. The phone goes straight to voice mail. Panic claws at my insides. We're about ten minutes away now. I wish I could take the wheel. The driver seems to be purposely going slower since having words with Fahad.

Finally, after what seems like forever, we turn onto my street. My mouth drops open.

The newly fallen snow is painted red from the lights of the police cars and ambulances outside our townhouse. A crowd of people is already gathering, and I can see emergency workers moving them away from our front door.

"Holy shit," the taxi driver says. "What the hell's gone on here?"

"This is our party," Fahad says sarcastically. "So you can stick your tip, eh?"

I jump out as soon as the taxi slows and begin to run toward the house. A police officer catches me in his arms. Someone is screaming over and over. It's so loud I can't think. I wish they'd shut up.

"Calm down," the officer says sharply. "You can't go near there. It's a crime scene." I stop struggling. The screaming has also stopped. That's when I realize it was me.

"She lives there with her mom and brother. He called us about a half hour ago from the bathroom, where he was hiding from their mom's boyfriend." Fahad's beside me now.

The officer's face drops. "Yes, we have the little boy, your brother. He's over in the ambulance right now."

"Is he okay?" I ask. "Is my mom okay?" Fahad puts his arm around me and holds me close.

The officer begins to walk with us toward the ambulance. "I'm Officer Lam," he says, handing me a business card that I stuff it in the pocket of my coat. "Physically, your brother's not hurt, other than a couple of deep scratches. But he's in shock right now. Do you have any next of kin in the city?"

I nod. "My nan…our grandmother. I've been staying with her the last few nights."

"We'll need to get a hold of her. Your brother is going to be taken to SickKids for assessment and questioning. Depending on what we find out, he'll either be admitted or released into your grandmother's care while we investigate. Your mother's been taken to a nearby hospital. She's got a pretty bad concussion and appears to have a broken jaw." The officer pauses. "I'm sorry, I know this is a lot, but we'll need to ask you a few questions about your family life as well. We'll have trauma counselors available for you and your brother."

"My nan is on her way here right now," I say. "She should be here any minute." I realize my toes are completely numb with cold.

"I'm not sure we'll be able to wait for her, but one of our cruisers will take the two of you to SickKids." Officer Lam turns to Fahad. "I take it you're not a blood relative."

"That's kind of obvious," Fahad fires back. Seeing the officer's unimpressed reaction, he quickly adds, "No, I'm Lizzie's boyfriend. But I'd like to stay with her if I can."

"You can stay until her grandmother gets here, and then we'll get an officer to take you home."

"No, thanks," Fahad says, holding his hands up, palms forward. "There's no way I'm having my parents see a police cruiser dropping me off on a Saturday night. I'll be in Lahore riding a camel by next week if that happens. I can find my own way home. Appreciate the offer though."

Officer Lam turns to me. The look on his face is serious. "There's one more thing you need to know before seeing your brother," he says. "Your stepfather is deceased…Charlie killed him this evening."

"What?" I ask. My voice is tiny, faraway. "He couldn't have. How?" I look over at the ambulance, its blood-red light shining out onto the crowd gathering behind the yellow police tape.

"Lizzie, I know this is a lot to take in," Officer Lam says, his voice thick with sympathy. He motions for a paramedic carrying a silver blanket to come over.

"I need to see him," I say, breaking into a run before either Officer Lam or Fahad can open their mouths to protest. The cold air burns my lungs as I gulp it down. I reach the side of the ambulance and dash to the back doors.

They're open. Charlie is huddled on a stretcher inside, wrapped like a takeout burrito in one of those silver-foil blankets. A paramedic is monitoring him, and a female police officer is writing something in her notepad.

"Charlie!" I stop, my Converse sneakers skidding in the icy slush.

The police officer's head snaps up. She throws her arm out to block me. "You can't be here," she says.

"The hell I can't be," I growl at her, pushing her arm aside and jumping into the back of the ambulance. "That's my baby brother."

Charlie looks at me, his eyes wide and shining with tears. "Lizzie," he says, his voice barely a whisper. "Dean won't hurt you anymore. I did a really bad thing. Really bad. But he won't hurt you. Or Mom. Or Trixie. He'll never hurt us again." There's a flatness to his voice and a blank look to his eyes that's scaring me. The words tumble from his lips with the emotion of a robot.

I throw my arms around him. "It's okay, buddy," I say. "It's all going to be okay."

The thing is, I don't know if anything will ever be okay again.

Chapter Seventeen

"Hey, Lizzie," Kayla says, taking a seat beside me. Putting down her Starbucks cup, she takes off her army jacket, shakes out her long dreads, then turns to me. "Ready?"

"Ready as I'll ever be, I guess." I put my script, which is heavily marked with pink highlighter, down beside me.

"Girl, you don't get it, do you?" Kayla pretends to knock on my head. "Hello? You killed the audition. People are nuts about your voice. If all that stuff hadn't been going on last year, you would've had the female lead in the *Wiz* as well."

I roll my eyes at her and laugh.

For the first time in a long time, my laughter is fueled by happiness. It's been a year and two months since the night that Dean died. Charlie was hospitalized for a night due to shock, and then his care was transferred to Nan while the police investigated his charge of self-defense. My testimony about being beaten regularly and then raped by Dean made a difference. I had to undergo really humiliating physical exams to prove that I was no longer a virgin. Fahad gave testimony at Dean's trial to support that we'd never had sex, which helped.

When Nan and I got to SickKids that night, we found out that Charlie hit Dean in the temple with an iron when he broke into the bathroom. He was killed instantly, but Charlie took a razor blade to Dean's neck just to be sure he couldn't hurt Mom or me again. That's how the police found him—covered with blood and sawing away at Dean.

I worry a lot about Charlie. He's sometimes so quiet and withdrawn, despite hours of therapy and Nan and I taking him out to things like Raptors games and the movies. His therapist says it will take a long time for Charlie to get over the trauma. He feels guilty about killing Dean and sees himself as a bad kid now.

Mom no longer has custody of us. Children's Aid gave Nan full guardianship. Mom came for a couple of supervised visits before entering rehab. Things between her and Charlie seemed okay, but our visits were awkward. She wouldn't look me in the eye. I thought hard about what Angel said, and I figure Mom didn't love herself enough to get out of the relationship with Dean and that it really doesn't have much to do with me. Down deep I don't fully believe that yet, but I'm working on it. Her face is really messed-up, and she'll have to get loads of surgeries to fix it. Not only did Dean break her jaw and right cheekbone, but he also managed to knock out half of her teeth. A women's charity is helping to pay for all the reconstructive work she needs, and one of the national newspapers is following her story. I don't think she really deserves the positive attention, but I'm trying to let that go.

Maie's keeping both Chester and Trixie for now. Last month she finished her chemotherapy treatment for lung cancer, but things don't look good. Even though she'd just gotten the diagnosis the day I showed up with Trixie, she still took her in. Nan's broken down and told Maie we'll take both the dogs if anything should happen to her. I know Nan's heart will split in a thousand pieces if she loses Maie, but she'll never show it. Instead, she'll take the dogs into her place even though she firmly believes they aren't supposed to be there.

Fahad and I broke up about a month after that night. His parents, though not happy he'd kept our relationship secret from them, were very kind and supportive to me throughout the trial. Thing was, Fahad and I were never the same after that night. Everything that happened was just too much for us. Regent Park is too far away, and it was hard for him to deal with everything that happened between Dean and me. I started at Mary Ann Shadd, and it was a new beginning with new friends.

Personally, I didn't want a lot of ties to my old life, though I will forever appreciate Fahad sticking by me that night. Maria and I have stayed in touch on Facebook, but that's about it. I'm okay with it all. My new life is full of promise, and I've begun to love myself. Most important, I'm singing again.

Dad, are you up there? Guess what? I'm Maria in West Side Story*! And when I hit the stage, it will be all for you. Love forever, Lizzie.*

Acknowledgments

To Robert, my Mum and my Dad for all their love and support, as well as a massive thank you to my agent, Amy Tompkins, for all her hard work and dedication in helping this book come to fruition. I would also like to acknowledge the Ontario Arts Council's generous support toward the writing of this book.

Mary Jennifer Payne is a graduate of the Humber School for Writers' Summer Workshop in Creative Writing. She is also a Special Education teacher at Nelson Mandela Park Public School in Toronto, Ontario. Her writing has been published in journals, anthologies and magazines in both Canada and abroad. *Since You've Been Gone,* her first full-length young-adult novel, was published in 2015.

orca soundings

For more information on all the books
in the Orca Soundings series, please visit
www.orcabook.com.